THE MYSTERY OF THE VANISHING CAVE

John Bibee

InterVarsity Press
Downers Grove, Illinois

InterVarsity Press® is the book-publishing division of InterVarsity Christian Fellowship®, a student movement active on campus at hundreds of universities, colleges and schools of nursing in the United States of America, and a member movement of the International Fellowship of Evangelical Students. For information about local and regional activities, write Public Relations Dept., InterVarsity Christian Fellowship, 6400 Schroeder Rd., P.O. Box 7895, Madison, WI 53707-7895.

Cover illustration: David Darrow

ISBN 0-8308-1915-0

Printed in the United States of America ♾

Library of Congress Cataloging in Publication Data

Bibee, John.
      The mystery of the vanishing cave/by John Bibee.
            p.   cm.—(The Home School Detectives; 5)
      Summary: While attending Camp Friendly Waters, Rebecca, Julie and
   Emily discover a cave with ancient Native American tools and weapons
   but, when they return to explore, the cave seems to have
   disappeared.
      ISBN 0-8308-1915-0 (pbk.: alk. paper)
      [1. Caves—Fiction.   2. Indians of North America—Fiction.
   3. Camping—Fiction.   4. Mystery and detective stories.
   5. Christian life—Fiction.]   I. Title.   II. Series: Bibee, John.
   Home School Detectives; 5.
   PZ7.B471464Myv   1996
   [Fic]—dc20   96-16142
                                                                                          CIP
                                                                                          AC

16	15	14	13	12	11	10	9	8	7	6	5	4	3	2	1
08	07	06	05	04	03	02	01	00	99	98	97	96			

Chapter One

The Hole in the Ground

Nothing out of the ordinary would have happened that day if Rebecca hadn't spotted the unusual hole in the ground. The three girls were in a hurry to get back to camp from their morning hike. Rebecca Renner, Julie Brown and Emily Morgan were all in Firebird Cabin, and they felt that the Firebirds had a reputation to uphold.

All ten cabins were in a race to get back to Camp Friendly Waters, named after Friendly Waters Creek, which ran through the middle of the property. Since the girls had come over the big hill instead of going around it like the other campers, they were sure they would reach camp first, grab the red flag and gain ten points for the good ol' Firebirds.

"Hurry up!" Emily said to the others as they walked up the steep rocky side of the hill. They finally left the trail and entered the large, flat open area at the top of the hill. The clearing, about the size of two football fields, was covered with short rough grass. At the upper end of the clearing, huge piles of rocks and boulders climbed up into the sky. At the very top of the hill sat a distinctive giant boulder called Moaning Rock. Jutting out against the clear blue sky, the big boulder looked majestic and awesome. The boulder had a hole all the way through it which made a moaning noise if the wind was blowing from the southwest, or so the local people said. None of the girls had ever heard so much as a peep from the giant boulder, however.

"This is a great view up here," Emily said as they stopped to catch their breath. "You can see for miles. It's too bad the highway is so close."

To the north, in the valley below, the four-lane road snaked through the countryside. Near the highway, bulldozers and dump trucks moved along a dusty dirt road.

"It looks like they're building a new road into the camp." Julie took a swig out of her water bottle.

Emily nodded. "They're the ones making the big blasting noises with dynamite to clear out the big rocks. That's what Mr. Sam says."

"I heard one of those ka-booms the first day we got here," Emily said. "It sounded like a bomb going off and made the ground in camp shake. I wonder if earthquakes feel like that."

"Hey, look at this hole," Rebecca called to the others. She was on her hands and knees where the clearing stopped and the pile of rocks and boulders began.

"Come on, Rebecca!" Emily yelled. "If we don't keep moving, we won't get the red flag. You want to beat Shelly and all those girls in Coyote Cabin, don't you?"

"They're dying to beat us," Julie said. "Especially after Rebecca teased her about that snake in the creek."

"Shelly almost fell into the water, she was so scared," Emily added. "But she did find that broken arrowhead. She was really bragging about it. We need to hurry, Rebecca, or we'll lose."

Rebecca didn't answer. She bent over the hole, trying to see inside.

"What's down there?" Julie asked as she ran over.

"I don't know." Rebecca leaned farther over the hole to peek. The hole angled down steeply into the ground.

"I don't see any animal tracks."

"Me neither," Rebecca said eagerly. "You'd see tracks for sure if animals lived inside here, because the dirt is so soft. The dirt looks fresh, as if it was just dug."

"Do you think someone was digging?" Emily said.

"I don't see any people footprints or piles of dirt like someone digging with a shovel." Rebecca leaned farther down into the hole. Her brown eyes shone with curiosity. "I wonder what's down there."

"I do too," Julie said.

"Come on, Shelly and Bernice will beat us back to camp," Emily said. But Rebecca wasn't paying attention. She searched the ground quickly. She ran over to a rock about the size of a volleyball and tried to pick it up, but it was too heavy.

"Let me help you." Julie ran over to her friend.

"Let's take it to the hole," Rebecca grunted as they lifted the rock. Taking tiny, awkward steps, they carried the big stone to the hole.

"Let go on three," Rebecca said. "One, two, three!"

The two girls dropped the rock into the hole. The round

stone hit the soft dirt and then rolled down into the darkness. The ground seemed to rumble for a moment, then the sound disappeared.

"That's a deep hole," Emily said finally. "I thought I heard an echo or something."

"Me too," Rebecca said.

"You better watch out," Emily said. "You might scare a skunk out of there. Like the song goes, 'I stuck my head in a little skunk's hole, and the little skunk said, "O bless my soul, take it out, take it out, remove iiiiiiitttttttt." ' "

The three girls laughed. That was one of the songs they sang around the campfire. Singing silly songs was one of the best parts of being at camp.

They had already been at camp for a week and would be there another full week. Camp Friendly Waters was owned by a Cherokee family who were Christians. The two-week sessions were divided up for girls only or boys only.

Rebecca loved Camp Friendly Waters. It was her first time to visit. She and Emily and Julie were the only girls to come from Springdale this session, but other kids in their church had been there before. The three girls from Springdale all stayed together in Firebird Cabin, and there were seven more girls in the cabin from different towns and states.

Rebecca loved the outdoors and all the activities of camp. They could swim and hike and even go horseback riding. She especially liked all the sports and games they played. She was a fast runner. Her favorite sport was soccer, but she liked playing softball, basketball and volleyball too. She was sort of short for basketball, since she was only ten and one of the younger campers. But her quick speed and good ball-handling skills made up for her lack of size. Coach Linnell, the camp athletic director, said she was a natural athlete.

The day hikes were also lots of fun. Going up and down the winding trails between trees and rocks made Rebecca feel like an Indian scout. Mr. Littledove, the owner of the land, was supposed to give a talk at one of the upcoming campfires about the history of the Cherokees. Rebecca was really interested in learning more Native American history.

Like Emily and Julie, Rebecca was home schooled. All the girls had studied several units through the years on Native American history and culture. She had heard that Mr. Littledove would also show the campers his collection of arrowheads and other artifacts. Rebecca had a keen interest in old tools, weapons and decorations of historical value. She had been hoping all week to find an arrowhead, but so far she hadn't had any luck. Like the other girls, she had been envious when Shelly from Coyote Cabin found a broken arrowhead that afternoon by the creek.

Rebecca could be very determined and almost stubborn at times. She forgot about everything as she stared down curiously at the hole. She even forgot about beating Shelly and the girls in Coyote Cabin who acted snooty whenever their cabin won a contest.

"I really don't think it's an animal hole," Rebecca said to the others.

"Who cares what kind of hole it is?" Emily said. "Shelly and her gang will beat us back to camp if we don't get moving soon."

"We still have some time to investigate." Julie got a drink from her water bottle, shrugged off her backpack and dropped it on the ground, where the other girls' packs soon landed.

Rebecca got on her hands and knees again and peered

down into the hole. She saw small flecks of white stone. She picked up one of the tiny broken pieces.

"This is flint," Rebecca announced as she turned it over in her hands.

"So what?" Emily said.

"Most arrowheads are made of flint because it's hard and can be chipped away easily to make sharp edges," Rebecca replied. "This is Cherokee land. I bet there could be lots of arrowheads around if you knew where to look."

"Like this?" Julie dug into the dirt and smiled as she pulled a white triangle-shaped piece of stone from the edge of the hole.

"It *is* an arrowhead!" Emily said. "Wow! You really found one."

Rebecca's eyes widened at the discovery. She ran away from the hole and picked up a long wooden stick. When she returned, she began using the end of the stick to loosen the dirt around the edge of the hole.

"Maybe there's more." Rebecca eagerly dug faster. The loose dirt fell away in chunks and rolled down into the hole. The other girls found sticks and began digging at the edge of the hole too.

"There's lots of pieces of flint." Julie dug at the ground by her feet. As the dirt kept rolling into the hole, which was about a foot across, the area around the hole got wider and wider.

"Stop!" Rebecca yelled. She bent over and picked up a grayish piece of stone. She brushed away some dirt.

"A broken arrowhead," Emily said.

"It sure is." Rebecca smiled. "And look. Even though it's broken, it's bigger than the one Shelly found. I beat her! Wait till she sees this one. She'll turn green with envy. Of course, yours is the best one of all, Julie."

"I'm the only one who hasn't found anything." Emily made a pretend face like she would cry.

The other girls laughed and said, "Then let's keep digging."

The girls stood around the edge of the hole and began to pound at the dirt. The dirt edge kept crumbling away and falling into the hole until they had dug a wider and wider area around the hole—first three feet, then four feet. But the size of the original, inner hole stayed the same. All three pairs of eyes were trained on bits and pieces of rock in the falling dirt.

"Wait!" Emily shouted. She bent over and snatched up a piece of rock. She turned it over in her hand and frowned.

"It's flint, but it's not an arrowhead," she said sadly.

"Let's stay at it." Rebecca picked up her stick and pounded it down. For a few minutes the dirt flew again. The pit around the hole steadily grew until it was almost six feet across. There were lots of chips and pieces of flint lying on the dirt.

"I think we should stop, you guys," Julie said.

"It's a great hole, isn't it?" Rebecca smiled.

"But look how big this pit around the hole is getting," Julie replied and pointed down. "Dirt keeps going down the hole, but it's not filling in. I'd think it would start to fill up by now."

"Then it must be a deep hole." Rebecca shrugged.

"That's what I mean," Julie replied. She bent over and poked her stick down into the darkness of the hole. She waved the stick around against the dirt walls. "I can't feel the end of it. It sort of curves down under Rebecca's side and gets bigger. It almost seems like a tunnel or something."

"It's just a hole," Rebecca said. "Let's look a few more minutes for arrowheads."

"I want to find one since you all found one." Emily began digging again. "I'll be the only one without an arrowhead."

"I think we should stop." Julie stared down into the pit around the hole. "The ground beneath my feet vibrates when you pound your stick."

"What do you mean?" Emily asked.

"Come stand by me," Julie said.

The two girls walked around the edge of the hole to their friend. They stood side by side, six tennis shoes pressed against one another in a line.

"See if you feel anything when I pound my stick." Julie raised the stick and then slammed it down at the edge of the hole with a thud.

"Did you feel that?" Julie asked.

"The ground sort of vibrates," Rebecca agreed. She pounded her stick down in front of her feet. The stick dug into the ground, prying a huge hunk of dirt away from the edge. The chunk of dirt burst apart as it fell into the pit. Some of the bigger hunks of dirt rolled down into the black hole at the end of the pit. Rebecca hit the ground again.

"Did you feel it?" Julie asked.

"Yeah, it shakes beneath your feet." Emily hit the ground with her stick. "You can feel it even more over here." Emily struck the ground again a few more times in different places.

"Look! We're making a crack!" Rebecca pointed at the ground behind her. A small chasm had appeared in the dry ground. Rebecca turned and jabbed her stick down into the chasm. "Wow!" The crack in the ground quickly widened to almost three inches across and four feet long. "Did you see that?"

"It looks like an earthquake hit it," Julie said. "Too bad our brothers aren't here. They'd love helping us."

Emily hit the ground and the crack grew even longer. The little chasm snaked away from the pit in a jagged, uneven path and then circled around back toward the hole at the far end. Rebecca walked over to the end of the growing chasm and pounded her stick down into it. Before she could pull her stick back up, the ground suddenly shifted and then dropped.

The three girls screamed as they lost their balance. Emily bumped forward into Julie, who was knocked sideways into Rebecca, who was closest to the edge of the pit. Rebecca put her hands out to catch herself and realized she was dangerously close to the dark hole.

The other two barely kept themselves from falling, but Rebecca hit the soft dirt inside the pit with her outstretched arms. The dirt cushioned her fall, but she still tumbled forward as her hands slid downward. The small girl flipped and landed on her back. She felt dizzy as she looked up into the wide open sky from inside the pit.

As she struggled to sit up, she grabbed at the giant dirt clod which held Julie and Emily. As she pushed down on the dirt to raise herself up, the big chunk of dirt began to move again. It slid suddenly downward in the pit toward the hole. The three girls screamed again as they all fell this time. Arms and legs jerked and thrashed as the big shelf of dirt kept sliding.

Rebecca braced her foot at the edge of the mouth of the dark hole. The big clod of dirt shoved into her back but then stopped moving.

"That was too close." Rebecca was out of breath. "I'm afraid to move my legs."

"Don't worry." Julie struggled to sit up. "We'll help you." As Julie started to stand, the ground seemed to groan beneath them. The dirt walls of the pit shook, and little bits and pieces of rock and dirt fell down. The ground shifted and then moved again. The floor of the pit near the edge of the hole broke away.

Rebecca fell downward into the darkness. She didn't even have time to yell. The other two girls rolled forward and somersaulted down into the hole behind Rebecca. A jumble of arms and legs and flying hair disappeared into the darkness as the ground swallowed them up completely.

Chapter Two

Inside the Cave

Falling down through the darkness reminded Rebecca of going down a steep water-slide tunnel at an amusement park, only this time she was sliding on loose dirt instead of water. But it was almost as slippery. She twisted and turned through the darkness, her feet in front of her, her body lurching one way and then the other as she slid downward.

Before she knew it, she slid out onto a soft pile of dirt and stopped. Dirt was still falling down on her as she tried to sit up. The loose dirt was followed by Julie, who landed on Rebecca's back. Emily came tumbling out right behind her and landed on top of both girls. Little clods of dirt rained down on top of all three girls for a few seconds, then finally everything was still and very, very dark.

Rebecca coughed and spat out some dirt that had gotten in her mouth. She wanted to rub it off her tongue, but her arms were pinned underneath her.

"Get your elbow out of my ear," Julie said.

"Sorry," Emily replied in the darkness.

"Where are we?" Julie asked in a muffled voice.

"We're at the bottom of a really deep hole," Emily said.

"It seemed more like a tunnel to me," Rebecca groaned.

The three girls sat up in the darkness. Rebecca coughed again. This time she was able to wipe her tongue, which she did with her hand. But since her fingers were dirty too, she still tasted dirt.

"Yuck." Rebecca sputtered and spat.

"Is anyone hurt?" Julie asked in the darkness.

"My leg stings," Rebecca said. "I think I scraped it."

"I scraped my arm, I think," Emily said. "It feels like a rope burn."

"Speaking of burning, I think I may have some matches," Julie said. "I had matches earlier today for the campfire. Wait, I might have left them in my backpack."

The girls groaned in the darkness. All three backpacks were sitting up on the ground outside the hole.

"I hope you have matches," Rebecca said. "Please God, let Julie have matches."

Julie felt in each pocket of her blue jeans. Everyone waited in the darkness, hoping and praying.

"They're still here!" Julie said with relief.

"Great!" Rebecca added.

"Light one. Light one. I hate this darkness," Emily said.

"Hold on," Julie said.

"I'm not going anywhere," Rebecca said softly.

Julie opened the matchbook carefully in the dark. She pulled off one of the little cardboard matches and struck it against the rough strip on the back of the matchbook. The match flared into life. She held up the burning match.

Rebecca was happy to see the light, but frowned at what the light had illuminated. The three girls had fallen into a large dark place surrounded by rock walls.

"This looks like a cave," Julie whispered as she peered at the rough rock walls.

"I wonder if there's a way out?" Emily asked softly.

"Maybe we could climb up the hole we came down," Rebecca said.

Julie moved the match toward the hole. The match's flame grew smaller as it burned out. The girls were surrounded by darkness once again.

"I don't like this," Julie said. "I have a full book of matches, but they won't last very long in this place."

"What are we going to do?"

Julie lit another match. She held it up to look around the big room once again. Near her leg on the pile of loose dirt she saw one of the sticks they had been digging with. She picked up the stick and held the thinnest end up to the flame.

"Come on, burn!" Rebecca said to the stick.

"Yeah, burn!" Emily echoed.

The little match burned down until Julie couldn't hold it anymore. The tip of the stick glowed red, but it didn't catch fire.

"Ouch!" Julie dropped the match.

"Try another." Rebecca wanted to be as encouraging as she could in the utter darkness.

Julie lit another match. The three girls watched the small flame intently.

"Please help it burn, Lord," Julie asked softly.

"Yes," Emily added.

This time the tip of the stick began to smoke and glow at the same time. Just as the match was about to go out, the tip of the dry stick began burning on its own in a small, wavering flame.

"Hold the end down a bit so the flame burns up the stick better," Rebecca said. Her friend nodded and dipped the end of the stick downward. The flame crept up the stick and grew larger.

"Here's another stick," Rebecca said. "This is the one I was using. Help me light it."

She grabbed the stick and stuck the small end up to the burning tip of the other stick. The flame in the first stick burned brighter and bigger. The tip of Rebecca's stick glowed red, but didn't catch fire. Rebecca stared at it impatiently.

"This reminds me of lighting sparklers on the Fourth of July," Rebecca said.

"Why?" Emily asked. "These don't sparkle."

"But they take a long time to catch on fire like a sparkler," Rebecca said.

"I never thought of it that way," Emily replied. Rebecca held her stick steadily over the burning flame. It seemed like it would only glow red and smoke. Finally, the second stick burst into flame.

The two burning sticks allowed the girls to see their surroundings much better than they anticipated. The flickering flames cast eerie shadows on the rock walls. Emily searched the floor around her feet, hoping to find the third stick so she could have a light to hold.

"I guess the other stick is still up there," Emily said sadly.

"This is like a cave." Julie turned slowly around and held

the burning stick up as high as she could.

"It looks like it goes off in that direction." Rebecca pointed to their right at a triangular opening in the wall.

"There's an opening in the other direction too." Julie pointed to their left.

"What are we going to do, you guys?" Emily's voice was edged with fear.

The girls stood up carefully. The section of the underground cave that they had fallen into was like a large room. The rock ceiling was almost fifteen feet high. The tunnel they had fallen through came out of the wall behind them, about three feet above the floor of the large room.

"We're lucky we didn't get dropped down through a hole in the roof of this room." Julie looked up at the tall ceiling. "We would have broken some bones for sure."

The girls crowded up around the mouth of the tunnel. Emily climbed inside while the others held their flaming sticks to either side of her so she could see. She tried to climb up, but she could only take four steps before she began sliding back down.

"It's flat here at the very end, which helped break our fall, but the rest is too steep, you guys," Emily said over her shoulder. "And there's nothing you can grab as you go higher. The walls are too smooth."

"Do you think it would help if we stood on each other's shoulders?" Rebecca asked. She poked her head into the tunnel and held up her burning stick. The tunnel angled up steeply for over twenty feet and then turned to the right.

"It's too far to the top," Rebecca moaned. "Even if we stood on each other's shoulders, we couldn't make it to the first bend. And who knows how far it is beyond that turn. I don't see any daylight at all, so it still must be a long way to the top beyond that first turn."

The two girls climbed out of the mouth of the tunnel. Rebecca sat down on the ledge of smooth rock. Emily sat down beside her, letting out a big sigh. It was becoming obvious that they had fallen into a difficult situation.

"We can't just sit here feeling sorry for ourselves," Rebecca said finally.

"This place gives me the creeps." Emily wished she was holding a flaming stick like her two friends.

"It smells too," Rebecca added. "What is that smell?"

"Bats," Julie said. "Look up there, on the roof of the cave."

All three girls looked up. None of them had noticed before, but the roof of the cave was covered with hundreds of small, dark shapes. Some were crawling around slowly, disturbed by the sudden light. The floor of the cave was marked by little piles of white and gray bat droppings.

"Bat guano," Julie said. "That's why it smells."

"Guano?"

"That's what you call bat droppings," Julie said. "It reminds me of the smell in my Great-Uncle Fred's chicken house."

"Bats give me the creeps," Emily said.

"Me too." Rebecca stared up at the small creatures suspiciously. "They're squeaking. How creepy."

"Bats are quite harmless," Julie said. "They are really one of God's most misunderstood creatures."

The other two girls looked at their friend like she had bats in her head. Everyone who knew Julie knew she loved all animals. She liked snakes and lizards and was even kind to most spiders. Now they could add bats to the list of animals that she liked.

"Misunderstood or not, bats still give me the creeps," Emily said.

"Forget the bats," Rebecca spoke up. "How are we going to get out of here?"

Julie held her stick up into the air and turned toward the tunnel that opened off to their left at the far side of the large room. She started toward the mouth of the opening and peered into the darkness.

"This passageway seems to keep going," she said.

"What's that noise?" Rebecca asked. "I hear a dripping noise, like water or something."

"There on the floor!" Emily pointed to the far side of the room. "There's a stream of water."

"Sure enough," Julie said with surprise. "It goes right through this room, from one end to the other, out both passageways." Julie entered the passageway near her and started to go into it.

"Don't you dare leave us!" Emily yelled at her friend. "No one should go off wandering around in a cave unless they're with experienced cave explorers who know what they're doing. You could fall down another hole worse than the one that got us down here."

"Emily's right," Rebecca added. "I have a cousin who goes exploring in caves with his friends. He says spelunkers—you know, cave explorers—never go wandering off by themselves."

"I'm not going to wander off." Julie stepped back into the room.

"I think we need to stick close together," Rebecca said firmly.

"Well, I sure don't plan on taking any trips on my own," Emily added nervously. "How are we going to get out?"

Rebecca walked carefully to the other end of the big chamber. The open passageway was shaped roughly like a triangle. The small stream on the floor of the cave trickled through the three-sided opening.

"There's another room through this opening," Rebecca said. Emily and Julie joined their friend. Julie held up her burning stick so they could see better. The stream cut across the floor of that room and disappeared around a large rock. Emily and Rebecca looked up.

"More bats," Emily said in mild disgust.

"More guano too." Rebecca crinkled her nose. The dark, furry creatures wiggled and crawled on the ceiling as the lights of the burning sticks disturbed their dreams. High-pitched squeaks scratched at the girls' ears.

"I hope we aren't upsetting them." Julie looked up in wonder at the furry creatures. "They aren't used to lights like this."

"I hope we aren't upsetting them too," Emily added.

"Another arrowhead!" Rebecca bent down and picked up a gray flint arrowhead in perfect shape. It was smaller than the ones they had found earlier, but the tip was very sharp.

"Look, there's another one." Emily eagerly got down on her hands and knees and picked it up. "Finally I found one."

"Indians must have used this cave." Julie bent down. She searched the floor of the cave with her friend, hoping they would find some more arrowheads. For a moment, the discovery of old treasures made the girls forget they might be trapped in the cave. Julie and Emily got down on their hands and knees for a better look.

Rebecca walked farther into the room, following the stream. As the stream curved around a large rock, Rebecca followed it, looking intently on the ground for arrowheads. Beyond the curved rock, the passageway opened out into a huge cavern, so big that the small light of her burning stick couldn't light up the other end.

Then she saw a large, flat rock that was as long as the tables in the mess hall back at camp. Her eyes grew wide as she stared at the rock. Dozens of arrowheads and all kinds of stone objects were lying on top of the rock. Some of the objects looked like pottery, others like ax heads. Many were things she didn't recognize. She picked up a white stone shaped like an L.

"Hey, you guys," Rebecca said eagerly. She turned around and realized that the others were out of sight. She walked back quickly around the curved rock.

"Look what I found." Rebecca walked into the room.

"What is it?"

"It's something made of stone." She turned the object over in her fingers. "It's shaped like an L. There are holes in each end, and it seems like it might be hollow inside."

She held the white stone up closer to the tip of her burning torch for a better look. The other girls crowded around her. Each girl took a turn holding it and turning it over in her fingers. The sides of the object were marked with lines that looked as if they'd been carved into the stone. Julie put the object up to her lips. She blew through the hole at one end.

"It is hollow on the inside," she said. "I can feel air coming out the other hole."

"I've seen things like this before," Rebecca said excitedly as Julie handed it back to her. "It's an old Indian pipe, I think."

"It might be, but who cares?" Emily asked as she looked at the dark cave walls. "We each got something, but now we need to get out of here. We could be in serious trouble."

"Do you think it's really old?" Rebecca asked eagerly, ignoring Emily's fearful remarks. She couldn't wait to tell them about the other stuff she'd seen.

"Emily's right. We need to find a way out." Julie tried to subdue the fear she felt return to her stomach. "Later we can figure out how this stuff got here."

Rebecca froze. The white stone pipe dropped from her hand. She lifted up her arm and pointed behind the two girls.

"Maybe he brought it here." Rebecca's voice wavered with fear. The two girls whirled around.

In the flickering light of the burning sticks, they saw a pale collection of bones on the far side of the room. The circular rib-cage bones connected to the bones of two arms and two legs. The skeleton was sitting up, leaning back on a large rock as if it were a stone easy chair. The gray-white skull with holes for eyes and bare grinning teeth seemed to be staring right back at the three girls.

Chapter Three

The Skeleton

T hat was a person!" Emily whispered, pointing to the skeleton.

"Yeah, what's left of him," Julie added.

"He's been dead a long time," Rebecca observed. Rebecca and Emily both took a few steps back from the skeleton. But Julie took a step closer.

"Look. There's something on his chest," Julie said. The old bones didn't bother her as much as the other two girls. She walked over and bent down, holding the torch over the skeleton for a better look. Julie gasped when she recognized the object. The long, gray flint spearhead was embedded in the heavy sternum bone on the skeleton's chest. The point went all the way through the bone with three inches of stone showing inside the rib cage.

"This man was stuck with a spear!" Emily whispered. "Let's get out of here, you guys."

"Wait a minute, there's something in his hand." Julie bent down closer for a better look. The bony fingers of the right hand were clutching an object that Julie couldn't recognize.

"Hello!" a voice shouted from the next room. "Hello!"

The three girls jumped and yelped at the same time.

"Hello! Is anyone down there?" the voice yelled.

The girls turned and hurried toward the triangular passageway. As soon as they were through, they began to shout.

"Help, help!" they yelled.

"Are you okay?" the voice yelled, echoing down the tunnel hole.

"We're down here!" Julie yelled. "We can't climb out. It's too steep."

"Are you hurt?" the voice asked.

"We're okay."

"Wait and I'll be back," the voice yelled.

"Don't leave us!" Rebecca yelled. The voice didn't answer. The girls looked at each other anxiously.

"Don't leave!" Emily's shout filled the big room. Up above, the squeaking noise of the bats grew louder. The girls looked up just in time to see bats falling away from the rock ceiling.

Emily screamed as dozens of them dropped down into flight. For a moment, the air was filled with the furry creatures, circling and twisting and squeaking in high-pitched tones. Emily held her arms and hands up over her face as a shield.

The disturbed bats didn't seem interested in the girls. They whooshed around the room in erratic, jerking motions, and then suddenly the whole bunch of them flew through the triangular passageway at the far end of the room.

"O, Lord, get us out of here fast!" Emily said out loud.

"I sure hope that person returns," Rebecca said.

"I don't want to be stuck down here with a zillion mad bats and a dead guy," Emily said.

"Those old bones can't hurt you." Rebecca tried to sound braver than she felt. "I'm more scared of the bats. What if they come back?"

Emily stared impatiently up at the tunnel. "Please come back!" she yelled up through the tunnel, though not as loudly as in her last outburst.

"Catch this," the voice yelled above them. A few moments later, a rope appeared at the end of the tunnel. Emily grabbed the rope quickly. The end of the rope was tied in a loop about three feet in diameter.

"We got it," Julie yelled.

"Put it around your waist and let me pull you up!" the voice yelled.

"There are three of us down here!" Julie shouted.

There was a pause. The three girls held their breath, waiting for an answer.

"Only one at a time—that's all I can pull up," the voice shouted back.

"Who's first?" Emily asked.

"I'll go last," Rebecca volunteered. "I'm the smallest and weigh the least. If they get tired of pulling, it's better to pull less weight last."

"But I should go last since I'm the oldest," Julie said.

"No, Rebecca's probably right." Emily turned to Julie. "You should go first because you're bigger than me, and I'll go next because I weigh more than Rebecca."

"Are you sure?" Julie asked.

"I think it's the best plan."

"Are you ready?" the voice above them shouted.

"Not yet!" Emily shouted back. She gave the looped end of the rope to Julie.

Julie pulled the loop down over her head and shoulders so the rope rested against her lower back. She then reached up and grabbed the rope dangling down in front of her with both hands.

"I'm ready!" she yelled.

The rope grew taut, then Julie began to move upward. She tightened her grip. She leaned back against the loop of the rope and walked on the side of the tunnel as she went up.

"There she goes," Rebecca said as her friend disappeared up the dark hole.

"Hang on tight, Julie!" Emily called out in a wavering voice. Rebecca patted her friend on the back.

"I'm doing okay!" Julie yelled.

Bits of loose dirt and rock tumbled down the hole. Rebecca and Emily took a step back. They waited anxiously.

"I'm out!" Julie yelled. Her voice sounded very far away.

"Send down the rope," Emily yelled. The two girls waited again. Time passed more slowly than ever as they waited to get rescued from the bottom of the deep hole. Emily gave her stick to Rebecca, so the youngest girl held both burning sticks. The two girls watched the hole intently. The looped end of the rope finally dangled into view.

"Your turn," Rebecca said.

"You sure?" Emily asked.

"We already decided," Rebecca said bravely. Emily nodded and smiled. She pulled the loop around her waist and grabbed the rope.

"I'm ready," she called. The rope grew taut, then Emily

started up the tunnel.

"Don't forget me," Rebecca called out.

"We won't," Emily replied.

Rebecca felt lonely as her friend went out of sight. She held the two burning sticks. Shadows flickered all across the walls of the large room. She looked at the triangular-shaped passageway that led into the room with the skeleton. At that moment, she remembered that she had dropped the white stone pipe.

"I'm going to get something," she shouted up the hole. She quickly turned and walked toward the triangular passageway. Holding the two burning sticks out in front of her, she entered the room with the skeleton.

Without hesitating, she walked across the room. The white stone pipe was lying on the ground. She bent down, picked it up and stuffed it in her pocket.

She turned to leave but then stopped. She stared at the skeleton. She walked over for a better look. The room seemed so quiet. The fingers of the bony right hand were holding something. She bent down to see what it was.

"Rebecca!" voices called. "Rebecca!"

Rebecca stood up. She walked over to the little flowing stream on the cave floor and followed it around the curved rock that led into the room with the stone table. She walked past the table into the room. She gasped at what she saw. The walls of the room were lined with ledges which had stone objects lying on them. Other flat-surfaced rocks held stone objects as well. There appeared to be even more stuff at the farther end of the room.

"Rebecca! *Rebecca!*" the voices were calling.

"*I'm coming!*" she yelled. Up above, the bats on the

ceiling began squeaking and squirming. Rebecca frowned. Some of the bats dropped and began flying around the room.

Rebecca followed the stream back to the big stone table. She picked up a long sharp rock that had to be some kind of spearhead. She stuck it in her hip pocket hurriedly and kept walking. She passed through the room with the skeleton and walked through the triangular passageway.

"Rebecca, are you all right?" voices were yelling.

"I'm okay," Rebecca yelled as she hurried to the tunnel. The loop of rope was lying on the ground. She stuck the two burning sticks into the loose dirt near the hole and then picked up the rope.

"I've got it!" Rebecca yelled as she yanked on the rope. She pulled the loop over her head and shoulders as the others had done. She leaned back against the loop and grabbed the rope with both hands. "I'm ready!"

The rope began to move. The loop dug into the small of her back as she was pulled upward. She looked back over her shoulder. The two sticks burned like lonely wooden candles on the mound of dirt.

Rebecca held on tight. The rope pulled her up into the tunnel. By leaning back into the loop she was able to brace her feet and walk up the sides of the tunnel while she was being pulled upward. The hole curved one way and then another. Rebecca held on as tightly as she could. Whoever was pulling the rope was doing it fairly quickly. She kept looking above her, hoping to see daylight.

"Hang on!" Emily's voice rang out. Rebecca was happy that her friend's voice didn't sound nearly so far away.

Rebecca's feet suddenly slipped on the smooth tunnel wall. Her whole body jerked and swayed to one side, slamming her back into the wall. She heard a ripping sound. Something had torn her pants. She regained her footing quickly so she stopped swaying. Rebecca took a deep breath.

The darkness gradually began to disappear. After a fairly sharp curve in the tunnel, she could suddenly see a glint of blue sky above her. Then Emily and Julie looked over the edge of the hole. Both of them extended their arms to help their friend. They were smiling. The rope kept pulling steadily upward. Rebecca held on.

"You made it!" Julie said as Rebecca's head popped up above the ground. She held on until she was pulled all the way out of the hole. Rebecca took a deep breath, filling her lungs with the clean fresh air of freedom. The blue sky had never looked so good to the girl. Julie and Emily each gave her a hug. Rebecca looked around to see her rescuer.

The rope was attached to the saddle horn of a brown-and-white pony. A girl with long black hair and dark skin was holding the reins of the horse. She looked serious. Rebecca pulled the loop over her shoulder and head. The girl nodded and wound it up.

"Who is she?" Rebecca asked the others softly.

"She's a Cherokee named Mary Littledove," Julie said. "I think her grandfather is the man who owns the camp."

"She hasn't said too much," Emily added. "I think she's kind of shy."

Rebecca looked over at the girl. The Cherokee girl ignored the others as she slowly worked the rope into a tight coil.

"She said she saw us digging and then saw us fall into the hole," Julie said. "Her horse was down at the bottom of the hill, eating grass by the creek. She ran and got him and the rope."

"I'm sure glad she was there," Rebecca watched the girl attach the rope to the side of the saddle. The pony nibbled at the short grass beneath his feet. Mary patted the pony's flank and then turned toward the girls. She walked over slowly.

"Thank you very much," Rebecca said. "I don't know how we would have gotten out of there if it hadn't been for you."

"Well, I had a lot of help from Thunder," the girl said shyly.

"Is that your pony's name?"

Mary Littledove nodded. Her eyes twinkled as she looked at the girls. The corners of her mouth turned up in a smile.

"What's so funny?" Julie asked.

"I should not laugh," Mary said. "But all of you are so dirty."

Rebecca and the two other escapees from the cave looked at each other. For the first time they noticed the dirt on their clothes and faces and arms. They began to grin and laugh.

"You're really a mess," Rebecca said to Emily. "Don't you ever take a bath?"

"Don't you ever wash your hair?" Emily shot back with a smile. Rebecca reached up and touched her black hair. She crinkled her nose in disgust.

"I feel filthy," Rebecca said.

"We're all filthy," Julie agreed. "And we need to get back to camp. We'll be the last ones there. They might even be worried. We better hurry."

"But what about the guy down in the cave?" Rebecca asked.

"You mean someone else is trapped down there?" Mary Littledove asked with concern. "I only saw you three go in the hole."

"Someone else is there, sort of," Julie said slowly. Mary

Littledove looked puzzled.

"We found the bones of a dead person," Rebecca said eagerly. "And not only that, he had a big spear stuck right in the chest."

"What?" Mary asked.

The three girls quickly told her about the skeleton and the arrowheads that they had found. Mary listened carefully. Her eyes grew wide when they showed her the arrowheads.

"And I found this pipe," Rebecca added, showing her the object. "But that isn't all. I found a whole room full of this kind of stuff. I never got a chance to tell you guys."

"A whole room?" Julie asked.

Rebecca quickly told the others about the room with the stone table covered with old pots, tools and weapons. Then she told them about going back before it was her turn to be rescued.

"I grabbed a big spearhead, just like the one stuck in the chest of the skeleton." Rebecca reached in her back pocket, but her hand came up empty. "It's gone!"

"Your pocket's torn," Mary said.

"It must have torn as I came up the tunnel," Rebecca said sadly. "But I had a great big spearhead. And there's lots more stuff."

"This is very important," Mary said seriously. "I must tell my grandfather about this. Native American relics can be very valuable. If what you say is true, then we will need to investigate."

"Of course it's true," Rebecca said hotly. "Why would we lie about this? We all saw the skeleton, didn't we?"

"It about scared me to death." Emily nodded.

"And we found these arrowheads and the pipe down

there," Julie added, showing her the objects in her hand.

"We have to get back to camp and tell the others," Rebecca said.

"I'll go with you," Mary added. "I think my grandfather may be there, since he will give his talk tonight at the campfire if it doesn't rain."

The girls looked up. The southern horizon was filled with clouds. They were dark and looked like they could hold rain.

"Let's go!" Rebecca said.

The three dirt-covered girls gathered their backpacks and quickly strapped them on. They trotted across the stony hill toward camp. Mary ran to her pony and climbed on. She pulled the reins and headed out after the girls.

Though they were tired, the girls ran most of the way back to camp. The Cherokee girl riding the brown-and-white pony brought up the rear. By the time they got to the camp, they were out of breath. Dark clouds were blowing overhead and filling up the sky.

"They're already lining up for supper." Rebecca pointed to the mess hall.

"We're really late," Julie said. "It's too bad we lost the race."

"Yeah," Emily said. "But who cares? Wait till they find out about what happened to us."

"Yeah, wait till ol' Shelly and Bernice see the arrowheads and the pipe I found," Rebecca said. "They'll turn green with envy."

The three girls laughed. Mary Littledove climbed off her horse and hitched him to a tree.

"Can I have the arrowheads and pipe you found to show my grandfather?" Mary asked seriously. "I promise I will return them, but it's very important that he see these things and hear about what you found. I see his car over at the camp director's office."

"I don't know," Rebecca said slowly.

"It will just be until my grandfather can see them," Mary said. "He will want to know what you found and all about the cave."

"Come on, you guys," Julie said. "We'd still be in that cave if Mary hadn't helped us."

"My grandfather knows all about these things," Mary added quickly. "He can probably tell what tribe they came from and how old they might be."

The girls slowly handed over the flint arrowheads and the small stone pipe. Rebecca was the most reluctant.

"You'll be careful with them, won't you?" Rebecca asked as she gave Mary her pipe.

"I'll be very careful." Mary solemnly stuck them in the pockets of her jeans.

"The pipe belongs to me, remember." Rebecca frowned. Mary nodded.

"Let's go tell the others what happened," Julie said.

The three friends ran over to the line outside the mess hall. As the three dirty girls approached the line, all the other campers stared at them.

"You lost the race," Shelly Herman announced loudly. "Of course, I figured you would. But you do qualify as being the *dirtiest* campers at Camp Friendly Waters."

"You can borrow my soap and shampoo," Bernice Jones added.

The other girls in line laughed loudly. Rebecca glared at Shelly and Bernice.

"Don't let them get to you," Julie whispered, seeing Rebecca's anger.

"You should hear what happened to us," Emily said loudly. "We fell down a big hole that led right into a cave."

"Yeah, and we found lots of arrowheads and even an old Indian pipe made out of stone," Julie said. The other girls stopped laughing and began to listen, even Shelly and Bernice.

"Not only that, we found a skeleton in the cave with a spear stuck right into his chest," Rebecca announced proudly. "And there's all sorts of other old things down there too."

"A skeleton?" Shelly asked. "Are you sure? Where's all this stuff you found? I bet your arrowheads aren't as nice as the one I found this morning."

"It's a lot better than yours," Rebecca countered loudly. "We found several arrowheads, and they weren't broken."

"So where are these great arrowheads?" Shelly demanded.

"They're right over there with our friend Mary." Rebecca turned around. Everyone turned to look where she was pointing. But Mary was nowhere in sight, and Thunder was no longer tied to the tree. Rebecca looked over at the camp director's office, thinking she would see the girl and horse there. But neither one was visible. The Cherokee girl and her horse had disappeared.

Chapter Four

Telling the Truth

"Where did she go?" Julie asked.

"I don't know," Rebecca said anxiously. "Let's go over to the director's office."

The three girls took off. Shelly and Bernice and several other girls in the mess-hall line ran after them. Rebecca ran all the way around the old house which served as the camp director's office. As she turned each corner, she was hoping to see Mary or Thunder.

As Rebecca came around to the front of the building, she stopped at the steps. Shelly and Bernice smiled crookedly at Rebecca and the other two dirty girls.

"She's not here," Rebecca said with confusion in her voice.

"She said she was going to talk to her grandfather, Mr. Littledove, the owner of this camp." Julie looked at the smirking faces of the other girls.

"Let's try inside." Rebecca ran up the steps and knocked on the front door. After a few moments, Mr. Harvey, the camp director, opened the door. He appeared very busy and upset as well. Through the open door, the girls could see over a dozen men in suits gathered around a large table. It was easy to spot Mr. Littledove. He was older and had longish gray hair. He was a full Cherokee. Several other men were obviously Native Americans too.

The other camp program directors were all crowded in the room as well. Mr. Burke, known to everyone simply as Larry, used to be a real cowboy and wrangler and now took care of the horses and taught the campers how to ride. Mrs. Jameson was a very tall, skinny woman who taught the campers arts and crafts. Coach Linnell was director of athletics, and Uncle Bud Wiseman was in charge of the camp devotional and Bible study program. They all looked at Rebecca quietly.

"I'm sorry to bother you, Mr. Harvey, but is there a girl inside with you named Mary Littledove?" Rebecca asked.

"There are no girls in here," Mr. Harvey said quickly. "And I don't really have time to talk right now. I'm sorry, girls. Mr. Littledove and his sons are here for an important meeting. So if you'll excuse me . . ."

"You mean Mary hasn't been here?" Rebecca asked.

"Girls, I don't even know a Mary Littledove." Mr. Harvey looked at his watch. "I really must get back to my meeting. Besides, it's time for you all to be at the mess hall for supper. I will see you at the campfire if it doesn't rain."

Mr. Harvey looked at the cloudy sky briefly and then quickly closed the door. Rebecca looked more confused. All the girls had heard Mr. Harvey. For a moment, no one said anything.

"Mr. Harvey doesn't know who she is," Emily said.

"Yeah, I wonder why," Rebecca said. "You would think he would know the Littledove family."

Karen Moore, the counselor from Firebird Cabin, walked over to the group of girls gathered around the camp director's office. She frowned when she spotted the very dirty Rebecca, Emily and Julie.

"The lost girls are found," Karen said. "I was worried about you when you didn't get back from the hike. I was going to form a posse and go look for you all."

"Karen, wait till you hear what happened to us." Rebecca ran over to the tall counselor. Karen, like Rebecca, was African-American, and all the girls in Firebird Cabin loved her. Karen always seemed to have an encouraging word, a warm hug or a big smile. She was a great friend and a good listener. The cabin devotionals and Bible talks she gave inspired all the girls to live out their faith in God. She was an excellent athlete and a good coach. Karen was about to start her senior year at the university studying economics. She had worked as a camp counselor for the last three years.

The tall black woman stared with concern at Rebecca's dirty hair. "You girls absolutely must have showers before you come to supper," Karen said. "Miss Minnie and Mr. Sam won't let you step a foot inside that mess hall looking like that. What on earth happened to you?"

All three girls started to talk at once, trying to tell about the cave and arrowheads and the skeleton. The dinner bell rang at that moment. Mr. Sam, wearing his serving apron, stood outside the mess hall ringing the bell.

"Whoa, whoa!" Karen said. "Hold on. Too many are talking at once, and supper is about to begin. You girls go get cleaned up as fast as you can and come to the mess hall. I've got to go sit at our table with the rest of our cabin."

"Wait till you hear what happened, Karen," Rebecca said eagerly. "You won't believe it."

"I don't believe it either." Shelly was wearing another smirk. The other girls around Shelly giggled.

"It's all true," Julie said defensively.

"Well, tell me about it after you're clean," Karen said. "It makes my skin crawl to see that much dirt on one head."

The other girls laughed. Rebecca touched her head self-consciously.

"You better hurry up too," Karen added. "If you're late, Miss Minnie will close up shop, and you won't get anything to eat."

"Could you get us our plates and save them?" Julie asked.

"You know Miss Minnie won't allow that," Karen said. "One tray, one person. That's the rule."

"Let's go, you guys," Emily said to Julie and Rebecca. The three girls ran toward their cabin. They all knew how strict Miss Minnie was about the rule.

"Don't fall in any more holes!" Shelly shouted after them.

Thirty minutes later, much cleaner versions of Rebecca, Emily and Julie ran to the mess hall. All the other campers stared as the three late girls got their trays and silverware. Since it was past six o'clock, Rebecca was surprised to see that the counter was still open.

"I was about to close up shop." Mr. Sam stood behind the big pans of steaming food. "I heard you girls had quite an adventure."

"Sounds pretty wild to me," Miss Minnie said skeptically. Miss Minnie and Mr. Sam were married, and this was their first summer working at the camp. They ran the mess hall. Mr. Sam was also the handyman around the camp. He fixed stopped-up sinks, kept the pool clean and did a variety of other jobs. He ran the tractor on the hayrides. And at mealtime he helped serve the food. Miss Minnie was the camp cook, and a good one. Both of them were stocky and had gray hair which was always covered with thin hair nets when they served food. Rebecca guessed they were in their fifties.

Mr. Sam and Miss Minnie Schoon were pleasant enough, but sometimes they seemed impatient and cranky, Rebecca thought. They were no-nonsense people, sticklers for rules and punctuality. They always closed down the big stainless steel sliding cover over the cafeteria counter at six o'clock on the button.

"I thought we would miss supper," Emily said. "I'm sorry we're late."

"Thanks for staying open," Rebecca added. Miss Minnie only grunted as she filled their trays with barbecued beef sandwiches, corn, coleslaw and potato chips. Dessert that night was cherry cobbler in little hard brown plastic bowls. All three girls took a carton of chocolate milk for their drink.

"We made an exception tonight," Mr. Sam said. "I want to hear all about this cave or hole you fell into. You girls go sit down and we'll join you."

"It's like we are celebrities or heroes," Julie whispered to the other girls as they headed toward the table that held the rest of the Firebird girls.

"Yeah, Mr. Sam and Miss Minnie hardly ever pay any attention to the campers," Emily added.

Rebecca sat down beside Karen. The other girls scooted over so Emily and Julie could sit on Karen's other side. Most

of the campers in the mess hall were done eating, so they
gathered around the table. Shelly and Bernice, from Coyote
Cabin, were at the next table sitting beside their counselor,
Janet Crowe. Janet was half Cherokee and half Caucasian.
She went to the same university as Karen, but she was an
anthropology student.

"So what happened to you on your hike?" Karen asked.
Between hurried bites, the three girls took turns telling their
counselor what had happened. All the girls in the mess hall
listened intently. Even Mr. Sam and Miss Minnie stood listening
at the edge of the crowd in their white aprons and hair nets.

"And I'm not kidding, Karen, that skeleton had an spear
point stuck right in his breastbone." Rebecca finished up the
last of her chips. "It was really spooky."

"And you say there's another whole room full of these old
tools and pots?" Janet Crowe asked with interest. "You may
have really found something. With a find like that, the state
historical society would want to start a careful dig and exca-
vation for sure. This place could become famous."

"Really?" Rebecca asked. "That would be great!"

"Where did you say this hole was?" Mr. Sam asked.

"Up on the big hill by Moaning Rock," Rebecca said.

"Right past that big clearing where all the boulders and
rocks begin near the top of the hill," Emily added.

"I don't remember seeing any hole like that around there."
The older man frowned.

"Me neither," Miss Minnie said skeptically. "We were
walking up there just two days ago. Are you sure that's the
place?"

"Of course we're sure," Julie said. "We can take you there
right now if you want."

"Yeah," Rebecca added.

"I don't think so." Mr. Sam pointed outside. Water was dripping off the eaves outside the windows. The sky was gray with rain.

"Rats." Rebecca watched the steady drizzle.

"I think what you said makes a good story to tell around the campfire," Shelly said finally. "You can tell that skeleton stuff along with the story about the one-armed man looking for his lost arm and other ghost stories."

"This isn't a story like that," Julie said defensively.

"Sounds pretty far-fetched to me," Bernice said. "Are you sure you guys just aren't making excuses for losing the race back to camp?"

"Excuses!" Rebecca said hotly. "Every word we said is true."

"Then where are all these great arrowheads you found?" Shelly smugly reached into her pocket and pulled out her broken piece of arrowhead. She held it up for the other girls to see. "Here's proof of the arrowhead I found. Where's your evidence?"

"Yeah, where are they?" Bernice added.

"We told you that Mary Littledove has them."

"Right, the mystery Cherokee girl no one has seen," Shelly said. "And Mr. Harvey, the camp director, said he never heard of her."

"She's Mr. Littledove's granddaughter," Emily replied. "At least that's who she said she was . . ."

"I've never seen her around here, have you?" Shelly asked her counselor.

"I guess I don't know her," Janet admitted. "But I don't know the Littledove family very well. They don't come to the camp itself very often. They stay on their ranch."

"Mr. Sam or Miss Minnie might know her," Rebecca said. "Do you?"

She turned around to see their response, but the older couple were back in the kitchen closing down the stainless steel cover over the counter. Rebecca frowned and sighed at the same time.

"They probably don't know her because she's a ghost, just like the ghosts in the cave," Shelly smirked.

"We didn't say we saw ghosts, Shelly," Julie countered. "We said we saw a skeleton."

"I know, with a big spear in its chest." Shelly mockingly faked a yawn.

"We did see a skeleton!" Rebecca insisted. She could feel tears of frustration coming into her eyes. The other girls in the camp looked at her with doubtful faces.

"Do you know Mary Littledove?" Julie asked Karen. "You've been a counselor here a long time."

"Actually, I don't know her," Karen said slowly. "But like Janet said, the Littledove family doesn't come over to the camp much. The grandfather comes and talks one evening per session about the Cherokees and tells about the Trail of Tears and other historical information about the tribe."

"So you don't believe in this mystery girl either?" Shelly asked.

"I didn't say that, Shelly," Karen replied. "I'm just saying I don't know her personally."

"Well, she exists, and she has all the arrowheads that we found," Rebecca said. "The cave exists, and there is a skeleton down there and all kinds of other stuff."

"Maybe she is an angel or something like that and came

out of the woods to help you and then disappeared," Bernice said. "I've heard about things like that."

"I believe in angels, but I don't think she was an angel," Julie said. "Besides, she had a brown-and-white horse named Thunder."

"Aren't there some angels on horses with chariots of fire?" Bernice countered. "That's in the Bible. If they had chariots, then they had horses to pull them . . ."

"I don't think she was an angel either," Rebecca said. "That's just preposterous."

"No more preposterous than your story," Shelly mumbled and then giggled. The other girls of Coyote Cabin giggled at Shelly's joke.

"Stop that!" Rebecca looked away from Shelly. She was not going to let Shelly make her cry.

"I didn't say anything," Shelly shot back.

"You might as well be calling us liars," Rebecca said angrily.

"Well, so far all we've heard is a bunch of—"

"Hold on, ladies," Karen said in a soft but firm voice. "I want everyone to stop right now before we start a shouting match. Christians don't accuse each other of lying."

"Well, she hasn't got any proof of what she's saying," Shelly countered.

"We can go over to Moaning Rock Hill tomorrow and find the hole they're talking about," Janet said. "In fact, I would like to see it."

"You mean you believe their story?" Shelly almost sounded as if she felt betrayed at her counselor's taking the side of the girls in Firebird Cabin.

"Why shouldn't I believe it?" Janet asked. "Why would

these girls make up a story like this?"

"I don't know," Shelly said glumly. "Unless they just wanted to make excuses for not winning the race back to camp."

"We aren't making excuses." Rebecca tried to control her anger.

"We'll check into it tomorrow," Karen said. "If it keeps raining, we'll be meeting in the lodge tonight for Ping-Pong and games. I don't want to hear any more accusations or counteraccusations tonight. It's not the way Jesus taught us to act toward one another. Who can tell me where it says that 'love hopes all things and believes all things'?"

"First Corinthians thirteen, the love chapter," Julie said quickly, smiling.

"That's correct," Karen said. "Now put away your trays, and let's go have some fun."

The crowd of girls broke up. Emily hurried to finish the last of her food. Both Julie and Rebecca waited. Soon they were the only ones left in the dining hall. When Emily was done, all three girls took their trays up to the cleanup counter and headed outdoors. They stood under the eaves of the mess hall, hoping for a break in the rain.

"I wonder where Mary Littledove went," Rebecca said. "Do you think she is trying to double-cross us and steal our arrowheads?"

"I don't know," Julie said. "She seemed like a really nice girl. I don't think she would steal something we found. The arrowheads can't be worth much money."

"But that pipe I found might be really valuable," Rebecca said angrily. "I think she might have stolen it."

"Her name might not even be Mary Littledove at all,"

Emily added bitterly. "She made us look like fools."

"Wait a minute, you guys," Julie said. "We're accusing Mary without knowing all the facts, just like Shelly and Bernice are accusing us."

"Well, where is she then?" Rebecca demanded.

"I don't know," Julie said. "For our sakes I hope she wasn't an angel, and really disappeared . . ."

The other girls nodded their heads. They watched the rain, which didn't appear to be slowing down.

"We're going to have to run for it," Rebecca said.

All three girls covered their heads as they shot out into the rain. The lodge wasn't too far away. The large meeting room was filled with campers. Some were playing at the Ping-Pong and pool tables. Others were playing board games. Some were gathered in groups to sing and play guitars. Other girls were just talking.

Emily, Julie and Rebecca stuck together. Soon they were in a fierce Ping-Pong match with the other girls in their cabin. No one said anything about the cave or skeleton or Mary Littledove, and Rebecca was happy to avoid the subject. At nine o'clock, everyone started back to their cabins.

Rebecca talked excitedly with Karen as they walked back to Firebird Cabin. They were the last two to arrive. Inside the cabin, the other girls were standing by Rebecca's bunk with odd expressions on their faces.

"What's up?" Rebecca asked. The other girls stepped to one side. Rebecca stared at her bunk. A dark wet streak ran all the way down her sleeping bag. She walked over slowly.

"What happened?" she asked.

"Someone poured a whole lot of syrup on your sleeping bag," Emily said.

"They left a note too." Julie pointed down at the corner of the bunk. A plain piece of notebook paper was stuck in the edge of the pool of syrup. The words were written in the thick scrawl of a red felt-tipped marker: *"Christians don't make up Big Lies!!! Go Home You Liars!!!"*

Rebecca stared at the note and then looked at her wet, sticky sleeping bag. A long string of syrup slowly dripped down into a puddle on the old wooden floor.

Chapter Five

Back to
Moaning Rock

The grass was wet and glistening the next morning. Rebecca walked out of her cabin with plodding steps and tired but angry eyes. Once again they were the last ones to the mess hall.

Some girls were still in line as they arrived, but Rebecca didn't wait. She walked across the room to the Coyote Cabin table. Shelly and the other girls stopped talking when they saw her approach.

"How could you?" Rebecca asked Shelly.

"I didn't do anything," Shelly said.

"I just bet you didn't."

"We already talked about this last night," Shelly said. "Karen came over and talked to Janet. I was at the lodge the whole evening. Ask Bernice."

"She was with me the whole time," Bernice said.

"Liar!" Rebecca spat out. "You're the only one around here mean enough to do something like that to me. You're sneaky like a coyote too. You're in the cabin with the right name."

"I didn't do anything!" Shelly's voice was higher now. "Ask the other girls. They all saw me. We were playing pool the whole evening."

"You could have slipped out when no one noticed," Rebecca accused.

Karen walked over quickly when she saw Rebecca. The tall girl put her arm around Rebecca's shoulders.

"Rebecca, we talked about this last night," Karen said softly.

"I know, but I still don't believe her," Rebecca said angrily.

"That's not fair, Karen," Shelly said indignantly. All the girls in the mess hall were listening to the argument. The news had spread fast. Everyone had heard about Rebecca's bunk.

"Well, *someone* messed up my sleeping bag," Rebecca said loudly. "And I'm going to find out who did, and when I do . . ."

"Maybe it was Mary Littledove," Bernice said, trying to hold back a giggle.

"Bernice, you're just making it worse," Janet said.

"Well, she's accusing my best friend of doing a dirty trick which she didn't do because she was with me the whole time," Bernice retorted.

"I want everyone to take a deep breath and remember that we are Christians," Karen said firmly. She looked solemnly at all the girls. Everyone began eating again. Karen patted Rebecca on the back. "Go get your breakfast."

Rebecca glared at Shelly and then walked over to the line.

She went through the food line in an angry silence. She ate her food quickly. None of it tasted good. All through the meal she kept looking over at Shelly and the other girls. Every once in a while the girls would look over at Rebecca.

"I just know they're talking about me and saying all sorts of awful things," Rebecca said bitterly. "Just look at them smiling and giggling."

"Maybe." Julie was also still upset by what had happened to Rebecca's bed.

"They'll change their tune once they see the cave," Emily added. "We'll have the last laugh."

"Let's hurry up and eat," Julie said. "Mr. Sam promised to use the tractor and the hayride wagon to get us there. I can't wait to see ol' Bernice's and Shelly's faces when they see the cave."

"I'd like to push them both right down that hole," Rebecca said. "It would serve them right."

The three girls laughed. When they saw Karen looking at them, they quickly stopped laughing.

"Well, I wouldn't really shove them down the hole," Rebecca said finally. "But I sure would think about it."

The other girls nodded and smiled. They finished eating as quickly as they could. All the Firebird girls as well as most of the Coyote Cabin girls wanted to ride the hay wagon over to Moaning Rock to see the hole and cave.

Once they were outside, the girls waited impatiently over at the barn. The Firebird Cabin girls stuck together, as did Shelly and the Coyote Cabin girls. Finally Mr. Sam drove the old gray tractor out of the barn, pulling the wooden hay wagon.

"You ladies ready to go find that cave?" The old man

slowed down the chugging tractor.

"I can't wait." Rebecca pulled herself quickly up over the smooth wooden sides of the wagon. Bales of hay were tied together with twine in long rows on the wagon, forming long benchlike seats. All the girls found a spot. Karen and Janet were the last ones to sit down.

"This tractor goes too slow," Rebecca said as the wagon creaked along. "Can't you go faster?"

Mr. Sam didn't seem to hear her.

"We'll get there soon enough," Karen said. "I had Mr. Sam bring a coil of rope too and some flashlights. Janet and I might go down the hole and check out the cave if it looks safe enough."

"Can we come?" Rebecca asked eagerly.

"No, you can't come," the tall woman replied with a laugh. "Your mom and dad would get real upset if they knew we were letting you go down into an unexplored cave. They'll be upset enough as it is when they find out about you falling down that hole."

"They won't care," Rebecca said. "It was an accident. Besides, back home in Springdale we're known as the Home School Detectives. We've been in dangerous spots before and helped solve other mysteries."

"That's right, Karen," Julie said. "We're used to investigating things."

"I got trapped in a garbage truck once," Rebecca said.

"A garbage truck?" Karen asked in shock.

"That's right," Rebecca insisted. "We even got dumped out at the dump. But it didn't really hurt."

"Well, I'm glad for that," Karen said with a big smile. "I heard about some of your adventures from Emily."

"What will it hurt for us to go down into the cave again?" Rebecca asked. "I mean, we've already been down there. We can make sure you and Janet don't get lost."

"Yeah," Emily added. "We could be your cave guides. Just like those guides at Carlsbad Caverns."

"We don't need any guides, because we just want to take a short peek," Karen replied.

As the tractor and wagonload of girls entered the woods, they began singing a camp song about John Jacob Jingle Heimmer Smith. They sang each verse more and more softly, but then shouted out the chorus at the end. After that song, they sang some choruses of praise and worship. Karen sang out with her beautiful voice.

"Our God is an awesome God, that's for sure," Karen said as they finished a song. "A gorgeous morning like this makes me want to sing all day."

"Me too," Rebecca said. Singing the worship choruses made her forget the bad feelings about her bunk and the mean note. All the girls kept singing as they bumped along on the old wagon down the two-rut dirt road that led through the woods to Moaning Rock Hill.

When they entered the flat clearing, Rebecca stopped singing. Mr. Sam drove the old tractor straight toward the boulders at the top of the hill. The rest of the girls began to talk and point.

"We're almost there." Rebecca was ready to jump off the slow wagon and run, but Mr. Sam had strict rules about jumping on or off the wagon when it was moving.

About twenty yards away from the boulders, he turned the old wagon in a slow curve. When the side of the wagon was facing the top of the hill, he cut off the engine.

Rebecca hopped off the wagon in a flash. Julie and Emily were close behind her.

"Up here!" Rebecca yelled over her shoulder. The other girls weren't far behind.

"Don't fall in." Karen began to run too.

Rebecca reached the edge of the rocks first and looked for the hole. She searched the ground. She ran to the right and then to the left.

"It was right over here, wasn't it?" Julie asked, searching the ground.

"Yeah, I thought it was too," Emily added. "I mean, it was right along here somewhere."

Rebecca stopped and stared. She looked at the wet ground. Her eyes traveled up and down the edge of the boulders, but she couldn't find the hole.

"It was right around here. I know it was," Rebecca said as Karen and Janet came up.

"Where is it?" Janet asked.

"It was right around here." Rebecca looked down at the ground. "Or maybe over there to our left."

"I don't see any hole," Shelly said.

"I don't even see any pit," Bernice added.

"So where's this cave?" Mr. Sam asked as he ambled over to the group of girls.

"I'm telling you it was right around here." Rebecca stared at the ground. She kicked a large rock with her foot.

"This is the place all right," Julie added. "The dirt under these rocks looks kind of fresh."

"That's probably just from the rain," Mr. Sam said. "We had a real gully washer last night, almost two inches of rain."

"I don't see any hole," Shelly said.

"Maybe it caved in on itself in the rain," Emily said.

"No hole as big and deep as the one you described is going to cave in on itself with a little rain," Bernice said loudly.

"Yeah, you said there was a pit around the hole," Shelly said. "You should see at least some sort of hole if there was a pit."

All the girls looked at Rebecca, Emily and Julie. The three girls stared at each other without saying a word. Bernice and Shelly began to smile.

"Are you sure this is the spot, Julie?" Janet asked softly.

"I think so," Julie said. "It was right along here. I mean, all these rocks sort of look the same to me. But it was a big hole, at least two feet across, and the pit was probably six feet across."

Rebecca walked quickly along the ragged edge where rocks and boulders met the open field. Emily and Julie went in the opposite direction. The crowd of girls stood in a group watching the three girls search. Mr. Sam folded his arms across his stocky chest.

Rebecca traced her steps back to the group of girls. She looked and felt very confused. "I know it was right around here." She was standing on top of the nearest rock.

"I guess we better get back to camp," Mr. Sam said. "I need to work on the showers in Eagle Cabin this morning."

"Something's not right," Rebecca said softly.

"You can say that again," Shelly said with disgust.

"Are you sure this is the right hill?" Karen asked.

"There's only one Moaning Rock Hill," Julie said in exasperation. "This is the place. I promise. We were up here yesterday. We saw those same men down there surveying and working on the road."

She pointed down at the moving bulldozers and trucks. Karen and the others looked down the hill. All of a sudden, they saw a puff of smoke and dirt rise into the air. The ground shook. A few seconds later, a large boom echoed across the valley all the way up to the top of Moaning Rock Hill.

"They're blasting again today," Mr. Sam said.

"This is the right place," Julie said firmly. "I'm sure of it. It was right at the edge of these rocks."

"I'm sure too," Rebecca added.

"Then where is the hole and cave?" Shelly asked. She looked at the girls from Firebird Cabin and shook her head back and forth as if she thought Rebecca and the others were crazy.

The three girls once again looked at each other with puzzled expressions. Rebecca felt her face growing hot with embarrassment. Julie stared at the mounds of rocks, a deep furrow in her forehead. The silence was long and awkward.

"We better go back to camp," Karen said finally. "Mr. Sam has work to do, and you girls have crafts this morning with Mrs. Jameson. Then later, Coach Linnell has our cabin in the softball tournament. We play the Badgers."

"Something is wrong," Rebecca muttered, shaking her head.

"That's the first true thing you've said all morning," Shelly goaded.

"Shelly!" Janet warned. Shelly smirked once again and then turned back to the wagon. She began whistling a camp song as she walked. The other girls from Coyote Cabin followed her.

Mr. Sam shrugged his shoulders and shook his head. He didn't say a word as he headed back to the old tractor.

The three girls lingered at the edge of the clearing, still looking for some sign of the hole. Karen sighed as she waited.

"We need to go," the tall counselor said to the girls.

"It was here," Rebecca insisted to Karen. "I promise you there was a huge hole around here and it led to a cave and . . ." Rebecca stopped speaking because she felt embarrassed and stupid. Julie and Emily were out of words too. Mr. Sam started up the tractor. The engine chugged softly. The three girls and their counselor walked without speaking back to the waiting wagon.

There was no singing as the wagon rolled slowly down the big hill. Rebecca sat silent as a stone, staring off the side of the wagon. Shelly and Bernice were whispering and laughing with some other girls from Coyote Cabin.

As the tractor and old wagon rolled into the woods, Mary Littledove stepped from behind the large boulder at the top of the hill. Her long black hair moved slightly in the morning breeze as she watched the slow wagon pull out of sight.

Chapter Six

At the
Littledove
Ranch

The ride back to camp seemed to take forever. More than once Rebecca's eyes filled with tears as she heard the other girls talking and laughing. She knew they had to be talking about her. She and Julie and Emily didn't want to talk.

"This has to be the worst day of my life," Rebecca said to her two friends as the wagon pulled up by the barn. The other girls hopped off quickly and ran toward their cabins. Only Karen stayed with the girls. After Rebecca and the others got off, Mr. Sam drove the wagon back into the barn.

"We have to find Mary Littledove," Julie said after a long silence. "She's the only one who can verify our story."

"But where do we look for her?" Rebecca asked. "I'd like to wring her neck for running off the way she did."

"We could go over to the Littledove ranch house and see if she's there," Karen said.

"Could we, Karen?" Rebecca asked excitedly. "That would be great. You've got to help us find her. She's the only other person who knows what really happened."

"Let me go check with Mr. Harvey," Karen said. "Maybe Janet can cover for me while we're gone."

Karen walked over to the camp director's office. She went inside and shut the door behind her.

"Everyone in this whole camp will hear that we didn't find the hole and cave this morning," Julie said sadly.

"Shelly and Bernice will be blabbing about it to everyone they see," Rebecca said angrily. "I just hate her."

"Rebecca!" Emily said.

"Well, I do," Rebecca said. "I don't care if I'm not supposed to or not. Look what she did to my sleeping bag."

"She said she didn't do it," Julie said.

"Who else would do something like that?" Rebecca demanded. "She's mean and really sneaky, and I just know she did it."

"Well, somebody did it, there's no doubt about that," Julie replied. "I heard Karen tell Janet that Miss Minnie said a jar of syrup was missing from the kitchen pantry. She keeps a strict inventory of all the food."

"Well, we know where they got it," Rebecca said. "Now we just have to catch them and Mary Littledove. I'd like to teach both of them a lesson."

"Maybe Mary did it, like Bernice said," Emily pondered.

"I suppose it could be her, but why would she do that?"

Julie asked. "I thought she seemed like such a nice girl."

"You think everyone is nice," Rebecca grunted. "You even like spiders and snakes."

"Just the good ones," Julie replied.

"Mary Littledove could be behind all this," Emily said. "But I don't know how she could make that big hole disappear without a trace. I still can't figure it out."

The door to the camp director's office slammed shut. Karen walked quickly across the field.

"We can go over to the Littledove ranch if we don't take too long." Karen walked up to the group of girls. "Mr. Harvey tried to call, but the line was busy. They've been having more business meetings again today. Poor Mr. Harvey is upset. Something is wrong, but he won't talk about it. He seems discouraged to me."

"Did you ask him about Mary?" Rebecca asked hopefully.

"He says he hasn't heard of her, but he also said he doesn't know all the Littledove family." Karen walked quickly around the barn toward the dirt road that led through the southern part of the camp. The three girls had to trot to keep up with her long steps.

"So she may really be part of the family?" Julie asked.

"She could be," Karen nodded. "The Littledoves are a large family, five sons and two daughters. But not all of them live on this property. Right now, all of them are here because of business. The Littledoves are thinking of making some changes."

"What kind of changes?" Rebecca asked as they entered the woods. Karen left the road and got on a dirt path lined with white rocks. The three girls were right behind her.

"Well, there's some kind of disagreement about this property," Karen said.

"Maybe that's why there are surveyors and road crews over by Moaning Rock Hill," Julie said. "Maybe there's some kind of border dispute or something."

"I don't know about that," Karen replied. "But Mr. Harvey said they may close down the camp."

"Close the camp?" Julie asked with astonishment. "But why?"

"Mr. Harvey said he couldn't say because the Littledoves want to keep it private for right now until they make up their minds about what they're going to do," the tall counselor said. The path broke into three different directions at that point. Karen took the middle path.

"Are you sure you know where you're going?" Emily asked.

"Sure I do," Karen responded. "I've jogged out here lots of times."

The girls walked and talked all the way through the woods, speculating on all the recent puzzling events. Karen mostly listened as the three younger girls talked. As the path led out of the woods into an open area, the girls saw the Littledove ranch house. It was surrounded by a long wooden-rail fence. Several horses grazed contentedly beyond the fence.

"Look for Thunder," Rebecca said. The three girls looked for a brown-and-white pony.

"I don't see him," Julie said sadly.

"Me neither," Rebecca said.

Besides the big ranch house, there was a barn and several sheds and small buildings. Two camping trailers and a big RV were parked side by side beyond the barn.

Karen and the others walked along the path that ran beside

the long fence. They crossed the yard over to the house. A big porch and wooden deck ran along each side of the big house. They stepped up onto the deck.

"The front door is around to the right," Karen said.

As they rounded the corner of the house, they saw several cars parked in the long driveway. Most of the cars looked new and shiny and expensive. A new red Jeep was parked closest to the house.

"Wow, they really are having a meeting," Rebecca said, seeing all the cars.

Karen walked up to the front door and knocked. An elderly Native American woman came to the door.

"Hello, Mrs. Littledove," Karen said.

"Karen," the woman said with a smile. "Come in."

Karen walked in first, followed by the three girls. The house was big but simply furnished with old oak furniture. The living room off to the left was filled with men in suits. A few women were also sitting in chairs. As they passed by the room, Rebecca saw Mr. Sam coming toward them. The stocky man crossed the room quickly.

"We meet again, ladies." He nodded as he walked by Karen and the three girls. He went out the front door and down the steps.

"This way, please." Mrs. Littledove led them into a large kitchen. She motioned for them to sit down at a table. Without asking, she got four glasses out of a cupboard and set them on the table. Then she got a pitcher out of the refrigerator and began pouring cold water into the glasses.

"How can I help you?" she asked after she had finished filling the glasses.

"We were wondering if you have a grandchild named Mary," Karen said.

"I certainly do." The old woman flashed a big smile. "She's the third daughter of my youngest son, David. They've been visiting with us for a few weeks. They live in the next county."

"Is she here now?" Karen asked. "We'd like to talk to her."

"I don't believe she is here," Mrs. Littledove said. "She went off riding over an hour ago. She loves to ride horses."

"Does she ride a horse called Thunder?" Rebecca asked.

"Yes, she does," Mrs. Littledove replied. "Have you met her?"

"We sure have," Julie said. "And we really want to talk to her. Do you know where we can find her?"

"I'm afraid I don't," the old woman said. "She's quite a girl. She likes to explore and ride. Our ranch is so big that she could be in many places. Why do you want to find her?"

"She has our arrowheads and my pipe," Rebecca said quickly.

"She has what?" Mrs. Littledove asked.

Rebecca began telling the story of what had happened. Julie and Emily filled in other details whenever Rebecca slowed down to catch her breath. The old woman listened carefully.

"And this morning, Mr. Sam took us all up to Moaning Rock Hill, but the hole was gone," Rebecca said.

"We didn't see a trace of it," Julie added. "And the only one who knows about what happened to us is Mary. Only we can't find her."

"That is quite a story," the old woman said. "I wonder why Mary didn't say anything to me."

"She didn't tell you anything about us?" Rebecca asked in surprise.

"We've been very busy," the old woman said. "We have been having a family council for the past week."

"Have you ever heard of or seen any caves around Moaning Rock Hill, Mrs. Littledove?" Karen asked.

"No, I haven't," the old woman said. "This land has been in our family since the last century. And it was Native American land before that, only the people were not Cherokee like we are, but Kiowa and other tribes."

"You've never heard about any caves?"

"I'm afraid not," the old woman said gently.

Just then, voices from the other room got louder. Though the girls couldn't make out the words, there was no mistake that several people were angry. Mrs. Littledove frowned as she heard the arguing.

"I'm sorry," she said. "Our family is trying to make some difficult decisions this week."

At that moment, a tall Native American man strode into the kitchen, his face tense with anger. When he saw Karen and the three children, he stopped.

"This is Karen and her three friends from camp," the old woman said. "This is my oldest son, Peter."

The tall man nodded without smiling. He was still clearly upset. He appeared unsure of what to do.

"These girls say they fell into a big hole yesterday and landed in a cave under Moaning Rock Hill," Mrs. Littledove said.

"So you're the ones." The tall man showed no expression.

"You heard of us?" Julie asked.

"I've heard the rumors from camp." The man smiled slightly. "Mr. Sam said that when he took you all to Moaning Rock Hill you could not find the hole or cave."

"That's right," Rebecca said. "But Mary Littledove, your niece, rescued us. She has the arrowheads and pipe we found. She can verify our story."

"I talked to Mary last night, and she didn't say anything about these things to me," the tall man said. "She showed me no arrowheads or pipe."

"What?" Rebecca asked. "But we gave them to her to show your father, Mr. Littledove."

"You talked to Mary?" the old woman asked her son. She appeared surprised.

"She did say something about playing games with three campers on Moaning Rock Hill," Peter said to his mother. "But she said that they were pretending they were explorers and things like that."

"Pretending?" Rebecca repeated angrily. "She was riding her horse, Thunder, and she pulled us out of that hole that went down to a big cave."

"I only know what she told me." Peter Littledove looked skeptical and shrugged his broad shoulders.

"But that's not the way it happened," Emily replied.

"Why would she say such a thing?" Rebecca asked.

The old woman looked carefully at the children. Her wrinkled face was painted with a frown. "This is all bad business for our family. All these changes . . . I don't like what I see happening."

"These are good times, Mother," Peter Littledove said forcefully. Then he turned to Karen and the three campers. "I'm sorry, but we are having important meetings this week, and we are very busy," he said. "If you would like, I could drive you back to camp. I need to go over there myself."

"But what about Mary?" Rebecca demanded. "We really

need to talk to her."

"When we see her, we will tell her that you wish to speak to her," the old woman said firmly.

"Thank you, Mrs. Littledove," Karen said. Everyone stood up. They followed Peter Littledove through the house and out the front door. He opened the door of the bright red Jeep and motioned for them to get inside.

"We appreciate you giving us a ride," Karen said as they drove through a wooden gate at the front of the ranch. Peter Littledove drove very fast. Rebecca grabbed the door handle to brace herself as he sped around the bends of the winding road back to camp. He circled around and passed the construction crews working on the road. Peter Littledove waved to several of the men, and they waved back. Up above them, Rebecca could see the big boulder known as Moaning Rock at the top of the hill.

Circling around Moaning Rock Hill took awhile since it was so large. They crossed the bridge over the creek that wound along the long north side of the hill. The old wooden boards in the bridge rattled.

"We'll have a good road and bridge here soon." Peter gunned the Jeep up the side of the hill on the old dirt road.

As they climbed the hill, Rebecca saw a movement off to her left. Among the tall rocks and boulders she saw a brown-and-white pony. In front of the horse was a girl with long black hair.

"There she is!" Rebecca shouted.

Peter Littledove looked to his left and stopped the Jeep. All three girls scrambled out the doors.

"Mary! Mary!" Rebecca shouted.

Mary Littledove was over a hundred yards away. She

looked back at Rebecca and the others. In a flash she hopped on her horse and began to ride.

"She's going away," Julie said.

"Mary, come back!" Rebecca shouted. "Come back!"

The girl on the horse looked over her shoulder once and then spurred her horse forward. The brown-and-white pony and rider zigzagged in and out behind boulders and small trees as they rode away from the Jeep. After a minute the horse and girl were out of sight.

"She ran away." Rebecca looked up at Peter Littledove.

"There're no roads around that side of Moaning Rock Hill," he said simply. "And you'll never catch her on foot. I guess Mary doesn't want to play any games with you today."

The tall man got back into the Jeep without another word. In the distance another large boom filled the air, and the ground shook. Rebecca shook her head back and forth as she got back into the Jeep.

Chapter Seven

An Unfriendly Camp

By the time the three girls and their counselor got back to camp, it was almost lunchtime. Karen went over to the crafts building.

"I need to get my Bible from the cabin," Julie said.

"Me too," Rebecca said.

"Me three," Emily added. She laughed, but no one laughed with her. Nothing seemed very funny that day at all.

"I can't believe all this is happening," Rebecca said as they made their way down the path toward Firebird Cabin. "We should never have given Mary Littledove a single thing. She's a liar and a thief."

"Why would she do such a thing?" Emily added.

"I don't know," Julie said. "But I'm beginning to believe you are right."

"Beginning to believe?" Rebecca asked incredulously. "What more proof do you want? She lied to her uncle about us. She said we were playing pretend games. And she ran away when she saw us because she's afraid to face the truth."

"That pipe you found must be worth a lot of money," Emily said. "I bet that's why she's doing it. She knows we'll go home at the end of this week when the session is over, and she'll have all that stuff to sell after we're gone."

"That's a possibility," Julie replied carefully. "But that doesn't explain how that hole down to the cave just disappeared. What about that? How can a cave that big just vanish?"

"Who knows?" Rebecca pulled open the cabin door in frustration. She walked inside and stopped dead in her tracks.

"What's wrong?" Julie asked. Then she saw it. Rebecca's suitcase was opened on her bunk, and all the clothes were strewn over the mattress. As they walked over to the mess, they could see dark, wet syrup splashed all over the mattress and her clothes. Another note was lying in a pool of the sticky syrup.

"Why don't you fall down a Black hole and disappear, Black girl? Go Home You Big Black Liar!!!"

The girls looked at the mess in silence. Rebecca just stared. Julie put her arms around Rebecca's shoulders.

"I'll get even with her," Rebecca muttered in a soft fury. Her eyes got wet. "She can't get away with this again."

"We better go get Karen," Emily said seriously.

Thirty minutes later, they had collected all the clothes and taken them to the laundry room behind the mess hall. Mr.

Harvey frowned as he looked around the cabin.

"This may be our last summer as a camp, and I sure hate to end on this sour note." He shook his head. "We've never had anything like this happen at Camp Friendly Waters. I'm very sorry about this, Rebecca. And I'm especially unhappy that this person singled you out and made racist comments. This is totally unacceptable behavior. If we find the person or persons responsible for this, they will be sent home immediately."

Rebecca blew her nose and wiped it again. She had stopped crying, but she still felt a terrible anger burning inside. Mr. Harvey patted her on the back and walked out the door.

"We better go to lunch, or we'll be late," Julie said finally. Rebecca nodded. The rest of the Firebird girls were waiting outside. They all gathered around Rebecca, hugged her and tried to cheer her up.

"We don't want you to go home." Meghan McCamant tenderly rubbed Rebecca on the shoulders.

"No way," Sarah Sneed added. "We've got to have you for our talent night. You're one of the most talented people in our whole cabin."

The other girls stuck by Rebecca all the way to the mess hall, telling her all the reasons they wanted her to stay. Rebecca felt better, but she still felt anger stirring inside.

The Firebird Cabin girls were the last to arrive for lunch. When they entered the mess hall, it was already unusually quiet. By then everyone had heard about what had happened. Even Shelly and Bernice were quiet. The girls of Firebird Cabin made sure Rebecca was the first one from their cabin to get food.

As she walked to the Firebird table, Rebecca stared hard

at Shelly. The pretty girl from Coyote Cabin looked surprised.

"I haven't been near your cabin," Shelly said defensively.

"Yeah, she was with me all morning in crafts," Bernice added. "Ask Mrs. Jameson. She taught us how to make bead bags."

"You can fool everyone else, but you can't fool me," Rebecca said harshly as she sat down at the table.

The talk in the room grew louder as the rest of the Firebird girls gathered around Rebecca and sat down. The room was filled with whispers and furtive glances at Rebecca.

"I wish someone would tell those girls in Coyote Cabin to go home," someone said from the Firebird table.

"Yeah," a voice echoed.

"That's not fair." Shelly's face was flushed. "You guys are accusing me when I didn't do anything."

"What did Rebecca ever do to you?" Emily asked.

"Nothing," Shelly said.

"Rebecca beat her at Ping-Pong, tetherball and in the relay races, remember?" a Firebird girl said. "In fact, the Firebirds have beat you Coyote girls in most of the games. I guess that's why you're such a bad sport and have been out to get Rebecca."

"I'm not a bad sport!" the girl exclaimed. "I haven't been trying to get anyone."

Karen and Janet entered the mess hall. All the girls stopped talking when they saw the counselors. As Karen sat down with the girls at table nine, Shelly began to cry.

"They are accusing me of messing up Rebecca's stuff, and I didn't have anything to do with it," Shelly sobbed to Janet.

The mess hall began to buzz again when the girls saw that Shelly was crying. Rebecca looked over at the crying girl with bitter satisfaction, but she still felt angry inside.

Karen looked at all the whispering girls and shook her head sadly. She picked at her food.

"This is supposed to be a Christian camp," she said with a sigh. "It sure doesn't seem like it today. One rotten apple can spoil the whole thing, I guess."

"Do you think Shelly did it?" Julie whispered to Karen.

"I don't know who did what, but I sure hope we find out soon before everyone explodes around here," Karen said angrily. Julie was surprised. She had never seen her counselor get angry. "I sure am praying that whoever did those mean things will feel the conviction of the Holy Spirit and confess their sin so that Christian sisters in the Lord can live in peace and harmony and love. There's enough meanness in the world without having sisters in God's family doing hateful things to one another."

At the next table, Shelly stifled her sniffles. Bernice was patting her friend on the back. Shelly stood up and walked around the table. She stopped behind Rebecca.

"I am sorry about what happened to you, Rebecca," Shelly said softly. "But I promise on a stack of Bibles that I didn't have anything to do with messing up your stuff."

"I'm sure you're very sorry," Rebecca said coldly. Shelly, seeing Rebecca's anger, turned away. She walked back to her place and sat down. Her pretty face looked miserable and confused. Seeing the other girl suffer made Rebecca feel somewhat better, but it still didn't make the hurt go away.

After lunch, there was free time and then the usual afternoon of crafts and sports. Rebecca worked on making a bead-covered handbag in the craft shed. Lining up the beads called for concentration and careful work. She did okay for a while, but she kept thinking about the two notes and the mean pranks. The more she thought, the angrier she got. She stuck her finger with the needle twice and said a bad word softly. She frowned as she looked at her bleeding finger.

"God heard that," Karen said to the girl. Rebecca looked up in surprise. She didn't know Karen was so close.

"I know you feel bad, Rebecca," Karen said softly. "I would like for you and me to go for a walk and pray. I think God wants you to be able to forgive."

"I'll never forgive her," Rebecca said firmly. She wiped the blood off her finger.

"You don't know that Shelly is responsible for what happened," Karen said. "I talked with Janet. Shelly and Bernice were with the other girls all morning. She doesn't think Shelly did it."

"She's just sticking up for her cabin," Rebecca said. "Shelly is just really sneaky and Janet doesn't see it."

"I think we need to take time out to pray," the tall girl said. "Let's ask God for wisdom and see if we can understand how Jesus would handle a situation like this. Taking time to pray would honor him."

"Not now," Rebecca objected. She held her finger, which was still bleeding slightly. "I need to go get a Band-Aid."

Karen sighed. The tall counselor put her hand on Rebecca's shoulder. Rebecca stood up stiffly and left the cabin.

A half-hour later, Rebecca returned to the craft shed with a Band-Aid on her finger. She picked up her beaded handbag and started working again. Picking up the tiny beads with a Band-Aid on her index finger wasn't easy, but she kept trying. When the craft time was over, she stuffed the handbag and sack of beads into her backpack so she could work on it later.

The rest of the afternoon, the girls in camp played volleyball and soccer. The Eagle Cabin was first in volleyball, and the Badgers were first in soccer. But the Firebirds took second in both contests, ahead of the Coyotes. When Coach Linnell gave out the medals to the winning cabins, Rebecca felt better because they had beaten the Coyotes. She was laughing once again by the time they headed to their cabins to get ready for supper.

A parade of girls tramped through the wooded paths toward the cabins. Rebecca and Julie were walking side by side in front of the other Firebird Cabin girls. As they passed the Coyote Cabin, a scream split the air.

Shelly shot out the front door, yelling and crying at the top of her lungs.

"Snake! Snake!" she screamed. "There's a snake in my bed!"

A crowd quickly gathered around the Coyote Cabin. No one wanted to go inside, however. They stood outside the screened windows and looked in. Janet and Karen ran up and went inside. Janet took a mop handle and pulled back the covers on Shelly's bed. All the girls could see the large coiled snake lying right on top of the pillow. The campers stared through the windows and gasped. Shelly wailed as she looked at her bed. She was terrified of snakes.

Janet poked the reptile with the mop handle, but it didn't move. She poked it again, and still nothing happened. Then the counselor frowned. She leaned down slowly. She reached over and picked up the snake. Its long body dangled and bounced.

"Is it poisonous?" someone asked through the screen.

"No," Janet said with disgust. "It's rubber. A fake. Someone was just trying to scare Shelly."

The girls outside the window began to whisper excitedly. A few girls started to laugh, but quickly stopped because Shelly was still crying and shaking. Karen took the rubber snake out of Janet's hand and frowned.

"This is the snake from the prop room at the lodge," Karen said.

"You're right," Janet replied. "I thought it looked familiar."

"I'm afraid we've got a regular war going on at dear ol' Camp Friendly Waters," Karen said.

"Everyone go get cleaned up for supper!" Janet said loudly to the girls hanging around the screen windows. "The show is over. It was only a rubber snake. Someone else is playing a mean trick."

At suppertime the whole mess hall was buzzing with talk about the conflicts between Coyote Cabin and Firebird Cabin. Everyone seemed to have an opinion. The gossip and rumors were as thick as the baked beans on their supper trays.

"It was about time Shelly found out how it feels to be tricked," Emily whispered to the others at the table as she ate her hamburger. The other girls nodded.

"But what if she really didn't do those things to Rebecca's bunk?" Julie asked. "Everyone in camp knows Shelly is really afraid of snakes. Did you see how she was crying?"

"What about Rebecca's feelings?" Sarah Sneed asked. "No one should make mean comments about the color of another person's skin."

"Two wrongs don't make a right," Julie said.

"I'm glad to hear you say that." Karen sat down by the girls. "Tonight after supper, our cabin is going to gather to pray."

"But we are supposed to go on a hayride tonight," Emily said.

"The hayride is being delayed until we all pray," Karen said firmly. "All the cabins are going to take time out to do the same thing before the hayride. We are going to pray that this hidden war of gossip and mean tricks stops, and stops soon. What started out as friendly competition between two cabins has turned into something ugly and mean."

The girls could see that their counselor was upset. They got quiet and ate their supper quickly. Rebecca picked at her food. Karen watched her carefully.

"Aren't you going to eat?" the counselor asked.

"I'm not really hungry," Rebecca said.

"You aren't hungry for hamburgers, your favorite meal?" Karen asked.

"I guess not," Rebecca said. "I'll see you guys back at the cabin."

Rebecca took her tray up to the dish counter and left the mess hall. She went back to Firebird Cabin and lay down on her bunk. The churning feelings in her stomach wouldn't go away. The longer she lay on the bed looking up at the wooden plank ceiling, the worse she felt. She wished she could go home.

Soon she heard the voices of the others coming down the path. The cabin filled up with girls. Karen had the girls sit on the cabin floor in a circle. Rebecca stayed on her bed, however, because her stomach still hurt.

Karen got her Bible and read some Scriptures and talked about love. Rebecca found it hard to concentrate on what the counselor was saying. Her stomach hurt, and it felt like a boulder as big as Moaning Rock was pressing on her chest. On the floor, the counselor began to pray, and some of the other girls prayed after her.

Rebecca felt like she was going to explode. She sat up in her bed. She looked over at Karen. Karen looked back at her. A big wet tear dribbled down Rebecca's cheek. The counselor came over and put her arms around Rebecca.

"Can we talk outside away from the others?" Rebecca whimpered softly.

"You all keep praying while Rebecca and I go for a walk," Karen instructed the circle of girls.

Karen led the way outside. Rebecca and her friend walked in silence for a long time. They got as far as the baseball diamond before Rebecca began sobbing. Karen squatted down and hugged Rebecca tightly. Rebecca tried to speak, but her voice was too choked by the tears.

"What are you trying to say?" Karen asked.

"I'm sorry I did it," Rebecca finally blurted out.

"Sorry you did what?"

"I put the snake on Shelly's pillow, to get back at her!" Rebecca wailed. She hid her face in Karen's shoulder and wailed even louder. Karen held her for a long time. Rebecca's wails turned into sniffles.

"I know what it's like for people to call me names and put me down because of my color," Karen said. "But God still wants us to forgive those who mistreat us, just like Jesus forgave those who lied about him and misunderstood him. He forgave them all, and he even forgave those who killed him on the cross. If we don't forgive, we just get bitter and filled with hatred, and that hurts us even more."

"I feel so baaaadddddd!" Rebecca's whole body shook as she started crying again.

"I know you do." Karen held the girl until she was all

sobbed out. She took a tissue out of her pocket and handed it to Rebecca. The young girl blew her nose. She wiped her bleary, wet eyes with her arm, then looked into the face of her counselor. Karen smiled back.

"What do I do now?" Rebecca asked.

"What do you think God wants you to do?" the tall girl asked.

"I guess I need to tell Shelly what I did and say I'm sorry," Rebecca replied. "But everyone will think I'm awful. They already think we're lying about the cave and other stuff."

"You need to obey what you know is right in God's eyes no matter what anyone else thinks," Karen said. "I know that takes courage. But I also know that God will give you the courage you need, Rebecca."

"I hope so," Rebecca said doubtfully. She turned back toward the path that led to the cabins. "I guess I should go right away. I've been feeling really awful."

"I'll go with you," Karen said and smiled. Hand in hand, they walked back down the rock-lined path through the trees. The sky was getting dark. Rebecca was filled with fear as they knocked on the door of Coyote Cabin. Janet and the campers had just finished praying.

"Can you and Shelly come outside?" Karen asked Janet. Shelly seemed surprised to see Rebecca. The two counselors and two girls walked away from the cabin for privacy. Rebecca looked down at her feet while they walked. When they stopped walking, she kept looking down at her shoes. Finally she raised her eyes to look Shelly in the face.

"I have something to tell you." Rebecca's lip quivered. "I put the snake on your pillow today. I wanted to scare you because . . ."

Rebecca burst into tears. Shelly watched in surprise. Her eyes filled with tears too as she saw Rebecca sobbing. Rebecca thought for sure that Shelly would hate her. Instead, Shelly leaned over and put her arm around Rebecca.

"I'm sorry for saying mean things about you too." A big tear rolled down Shelly's cheek. "I think I did feel jealous that your cabin has been beating us so many times. I guess I let the competition get out of hand. My mom tells me all the time that I'm too competitive. And she's right. I hate losing. And usually I win back at home in our town in Indiana."

"Please forgive me," Rebecca asked.

"Please forgive me too," Shelly replied. Both girls sobbed and hugged each other.

"Now we're beginning to act like Jesus," Karen said finally. The two girls hugged again. Then the four of them stood in a little circle, held hands and prayed together. When they were done, everyone was smiling.

"We still don't know who played those mean tricks on Rebecca, though," Shelly said as they walked back toward the cabins.

"That's right," Janet said. "That's still a mystery. I have a feeling it must be another camper, but I don't know who or why."

"There are a lot of things that are still unsolved." Rebecca blew her nose. "But at least Shelly and I can be friends."

"Peace?" Shelly asked.

"Peace," Rebecca replied. The girls hugged again. Then Shelly hugged Karen and Rebecca hugged Janet.

"It looks like we'll have a great hayride tonight after all." Karen looked hopefully at the dark blue sky. A full moon had started to rise. As it turned out, she was right. The hayride over to Moaning Rock Hill and down past Friendly Waters Creek and all the way around to the Littledove ranch house was a big success.

The girls in Coyote Cabin and Firebird Cabin sat together and sang songs the whole way. Shelly and Rebecca even sat together on the way back to camp. No one talked about the mean notes or the rubber snake or even the lost cave.

Back in Firebird Cabin, Rebecca felt full of peace as she lay down to sleep in her bunk. Soon all the girls were asleep, resting quietly.

Past midnight, the door to Firebird Cabin opened softly. A figure in dark clothes holding a burlap sack moved silently across the wooden floor and opened the bathroom door. A hand holding lipstick wrote on the big mirror in the bathroom by the light of the full moon.

After writing on the mirror, the figure tipped the burlap sack open. Three thick, long snakes slithered out of the bag onto the bathroom floor. The figure in dark clothes backed out and shut the bathroom door. Without a sound, the person tiptoed by the bunks of the sleeping girls and went out the cabin door. The girls did not stir from their peaceful dreams.

Chapter Eight

The Hidden Entrance

Emily was the first person in Firebird Cabin to wake up. She walked groggily to the bathroom and turned on the light. Her bare foot stepped on the back of a big snake.

Her scream woke up everyone in the whole camp and probably people living in the next town, the other girls said later. Emily shot out of the bathroom and slammed the door. Within thirty seconds the whole cabin was empty.

Karen was the only one brave enough to go back inside. She opened the bathroom door a tiny crack. She saw the message written in red lipstick on the mirror:

"GO HOME, YOU BIG LIARS, OR ELSE!!!"

A large brown snake slithered out from under the sink. Another brown snake wiggled behind the shower curtain.

Karen slammed the bathroom door. She got dressed quickly and went outside.

The girls from Firebird Cabin stood by the front door shivering in their pajamas and bare feet. Other campers were running over to see what had caused the commotion.

"Did you see a snake?" Emily asked.

"I saw two snakes and another message," Karen said in disgust. "You girls stay out of there until I get Mr. Sam."

The tall black woman ran down the path. A crowd of girls gathered around Firebird Cabin. When word spread that there were real snakes in the bathroom, many girls went back to their own cabins in fear.

Mr. Sam and Karen came back down the path in a hurry. Mr. Sam carried a burlap sack and a stick with a hook on the end of it. The stocky man smiled at the shivering girls.

"I heard you had three unwanted visitors in the bathroom," he said pleasantly. He went inside the cabin. Karen waited with the girls. When she told them about the message on the mirror, Emily, Julie and Rebecca looked worried.

"Someone has it in for us," Julie said. "I don't understand it."

A few moments later, the big man came out of the bathroom with a bulging burlap sack. The sides of the sack moved and bumped. All the girls stepped back.

"Only harmless barn snakes," the big man said reassuringly. "Three big rascals, though. This kind rarely bites, and even if they did, they wouldn't really hurt you. They're probably more scared of you than you are of them."

"I don't think so," Emily said, shivering.

"I'm leaving this camp," Rebecca mumbled, shaking her head back and forth. "I've had enough of this."

"Me too," Emily added.

"I couldn't say I'd blame you after what you girls have been through," Mr. Sam said sympathetically. "This sure is a mean joke."

"Thank you, Mr. Sam," the girls said as the stocky man turned to leave.

"Glad to help you out," he said. "Now don't be late for breakfast just because of a few old snakes."

Mr. Sam carried the sack down the rock-lined path. The girls in Firebird Cabin rushed back inside to look in the bathroom. All of them read the message written in lipstick.

"Someone doesn't like us." Emily stared at the red words. "I'm ready to go home."

"And I'm ready to go with you," Rebecca said bitterly. "I've had enough of Camp Friendly Waters. I want to call my mom and dad and tell them to come get me."

"Me too," Meghan said. "This place is no fun. Maybe this cabin is cursed or something."

"Just hold on," Karen said angrily. "Someone is doing this for a reason, and I want to find out why. I'm going straight over to Mr. Harvey's office and demand that he do something about this. I don't care if it does interrupt all these important meetings. I'm not going to have someone scaring my girls half to death. You all go eat breakfast. And leave that message on the mirror. I want Mr. Harvey to see it."

Karen stomped angrily down the path. Rebecca and the others watched her go.

The girls in Firebird Cabin got dressed. Everyone was still on edge. More than one girl looked carefully under her bed before getting her suitcase out. No one wanted to grab a snake instead of a shoe. All the girls hurried to get ready so they wouldn't miss breakfast. Soon the cabin was empty except for Rebecca, Emily and Julie.

"Now I *know* it wasn't Shelly doing these things," Julie said as she laced up her sneakers. "She's more scared of snakes than any of us."

"That's true." Rebecca pulled her hair back.

"I'm glad Mr. Sam isn't afraid of snakes," Emily said. "He just went right in there and got all three of them."

"He's braver than me, that's for sure," Rebecca said. Emily had been tying her shoe, but stopped. She looked across the cabin as if thinking.

"What's wrong?" Rebecca asked. "You don't see another snake, do you?" Rebecca hopped on her bunk and searched the floor carefully.

"No, that's not it," Emily said. "It's just odd. When Mr. Sam came he said we had three visitors, meaning three snakes. But Karen only saw two snakes. How did Mr. Sam know there were three snakes in there before he even looked?"

"That's right," Rebecca said as she got off her bed. "He did say three."

"How do you think he knew that?" Emily asked.

Just then they heard a hiss at the screen window. All three girls jumped and yelped at the same time.

"Pssssstttt!" the sound came again. Rebecca was the first to recognize that the face on the other side of the screen belonged to Mary Littledove.

"Mary!" Rebecca felt herself getting angry immediately. She and the other girls ran over to the window.

"You mustn't go home," Mary said seriously. "You must help me!"

"Where have you been, and why did you disappear with

our arrowheads and my pipe?" Rebecca demanded. "You made us all look like fools."

"You have a lot of explaining to do," Emily said harshly.

"And why did you run away yesterday?" Julie added. "We know you saw us. Where have you been?"

"We cannot talk here," Mary whispered. "We must go now. I think my uncle may know about the cave."

"What are you talking about?" Rebecca asked suspiciously.

"Please come with me," Mary pleaded. "I will explain on the way. Bring your flashlights and backpacks. We must hurry."

"Where do you want us to go?" Emily demanded.

"Back to Moaning Rock Hill," Mary said. "Please hurry; we don't have much time. They will be signing papers today."

The three girls in the cabin looked at each other and shrugged their shoulders. They weren't sure whether to trust Mary. Nor did they understand why she was in such a hurry.

"What did you do with our arrowheads and my pipe?" Rebecca asked angrily.

"I had them in my suitcase, and they were stolen before I could show them to my grandfather," Mary replied. "My Uncle Peter stole them. Please come with me. I can tell you the whole story as we go. Don't forget your backpacks."

Rebecca and the other girls strapped on their backpacks. The three girls joined Mary outside.

"We'll go with you, but after that you have to tell Karen and Mr. Harvey and everyone in this camp that we aren't crazy," Rebecca told the Cherokee girl. "Everyone in camp thinks we've been lying about finding that cave."

"I'm sorry for the trouble I've caused you, but there were

reasons I acted the way I did," Mary replied. "We must go, before Mr. Sam or anyone else sees us. I'm not sure who to trust."

"Me neither," Rebecca grumbled softly to Julie.

Mary turned and ran into the woods as quickly as a graceful deer. The others ran after her, afraid she would disappear again. Once in the cover of the thick trees, Mary waited for them.

"You said you were going to tell us the truth." Rebecca tried to control her anger. "So let's have it."

"When we get to the cave," Mary said.

"Get to the cave?" Emily asked. "Did you find the hole? We were looking for it and it was gone."

Mary didn't wait to answer. She ran ahead of the girls through the woods. Rebecca and the others struggled to keep up. By the time they had gotten to the clearing near Moaning Rock Hill, they were out of breath, and sweat was running down their faces.

"We must be careful that we are not seen," Mary said.

"Who are we hiding from?" Rebecca asked. The Cherokee girl didn't answer. She headed up into the big rocks on top of the hill rather than walking out into the clearing. The three girls followed Mary as she zigzagged through the giant boulders and the rocks and scrubby trees. Soon they were walking underneath the huge shadow of Moaning Rock.

"The hole to the cave is down there," Rebecca said. "Why are we up here?"

"That hole was covered up on purpose," Mary said without pausing to explain. She headed down the far side of the hill among the huge boulders.

"Where is she taking us?" Emily muttered, trying to catch

her breath.

"I don't know," Rebecca said. "But it better not be some wild goose chase. I want some answers."

Mary Littledove picked her way down the side of the big hill. A huge bluff rose above them off to their left. The craggy orange rocks looked majestic in the morning sun. They kept walking downward until they reached the thick trees along Friendly Waters Creek at the bottom of the hill. They walked quickly along the bank of the creek until they came to a small stream feeding into the creek.

"This is the place." Mary started climbing back up the hill.

"Where are we going now?" Rebecca moaned.

"It's not far," Mary said. "We follow the stream."

The little stream gurgled and rippled as it cut its way through the large boulders and jagged rocks. Mary didn't seem to be at all tired. The other girls climbed after her.

"We're missing breakfast, and I'm hungry," Rebecca said.

"Me too," Julie said. "She can really move in these rocks."

"She's not wearing backpacks like we are," Emily grunted.

The Cherokee girl climbed higher up the steep hill. They were now in the shadow of the big cliff. Rebecca, Emily and Julie followed Mary around a huge rock, and the stream suddenly disappeared underneath it.

"Is this where the stream starts?" Rebecca asked. "It must be a spring."

"That's what I thought at first too," Mary said. "Yesterday I got this far and stopped. I thought it was hopeless. But I came back early this morning for another look. I'm glad I did. Follow me."

She walked around the big rock and started climbing through a narrow passageway between two more big rocks.

The girls climbed after her. Once they got to the top of the passageway, they saw the stream in front of them again.

"We're almost there," Mary said. The stream disappeared into a thicket of trees. The girls crouched down as they followed the stream under the low branches. When they got beyond the trees, Mary stopped and smiled.

The water poured around a large rock over ten feet tall. The base of the cliff was just beyond the big rock. Mary turned and walked around the rock. The other girls followed.

When they got on the other side of the big boulder, Mary was waiting for them at the base of the cliff. The stream was pouring out of a four-foot hole in the side of the mountain, almost hidden behind the big boulder.

"This hole leads into the cave," Mary said with a smile.

"So there is another way in," Rebecca said in surprise.

"You told me a stream was in the cave you found. I figured it must run downhill and come out somewhere," Mary said. "So I looked for the stream. But until this morning, I didn't know it would really show another entrance to the cave. I was afraid at first that it was just an underground stream."

"This is great," Rebecca said. "Now we can prove the cave exists."

"But that still leaves a lot of unanswered questions," Julie said.

"Yeah," Emily added. "Like where have you been all this time?"

"Yeah!" Rebecca added.

"I can explain," Mary said. "I wanted to bring you here first because—"

Men's voices echoed up the hill. Mary looked afraid. She quickly walked around the big boulder. The other girls looked over her shoulder. Down below they could see Mr. Sam, Peter Littledove and two men wearing construction hard hats. They were walking uphill along the stream.

"We must hide," Mary said. "Quick, into the cave."

The girl turned and ran back to the opening of the cave. Stepping into the water, she climbed through the dark opening.

"We can't let them see us," Mary whispered from inside the opening. "If they see us, they will discover the cave. Please hide. Hurry! We cannot trust them."

"I don't like this." Julie stepped into the tiny stream and climbed into the dark opening. Emily followed her inside. Rebecca took a deep breath and then climbed through the opening after her friends.

Once they were through the opening, the cave opened up enough so they could stand. The stream cut across the floor of the cave and disappeared around a corner into the darkness.

"I don't think they will find the cave," Mary said. "But since my uncle saw me looking over here yesterday, he must suspect something. Did you tell Mr. Sam about the stream?"

"We told the whole camp," Rebecca said. "But why shouldn't he know?"

"Because he's the one who closed up the other opening to the cave," Mary said. "I heard him and my uncle talking yesterday. Mr. Sam and some men from the construction crew covered the hole you fell into with a thick steel plate. Then they covered that with dirt, then lots of rocks and small boulders. They moved rocks by hand so they wouldn't leave any tracks from a bulldozer. The hard rain that night covered the tracks of the pickup truck carrying the steel plate. You were standing right on top of the hole and didn't even know it because they and the rain did such a good job. I saw you that morning."

"Then why didn't you come tell us?" Rebecca demanded.

"Because I didn't know at that time what had happened to the hole or what was going on," Mary replied. "I'm sorry, but I was afraid. Your arrowheads and pipe were missing, and I thought you would say I stole them. I felt like I had to find out what was going on before I could come tell you. Once I found out, I was scared. Some of the men my uncle knows are criminals and are dangerous. Please forgive me, but I was afraid. But when I found the cave this morning, I knew we could give my grandfather and the others solid proof of your story and of my uncle's tricks."

"I still don't understand why your uncle is the bad guy," Rebecca said suspiciously.

"You say Mr. Sam helped cover up the hole?" Julie asked.

"But why would they do that?" Rebecca asked. "Mr. Sam acted like he had never heard of the hole."

"That's because he's helping my Uncle Peter," Mary whispered. "Ssshhhh. I hear their voices. They're coming closer."

Mary backed away from the mouth of the cave. The other girls followed her example. They could hear the men talking outside. Mary held her finger up to her lips to tell the other girls not to speak. The voices outside grew louder. They carried well among the rocks.

"I don't think this leads anywhere," they heard Mr. Sam say. "This may be the stream they saw, but it's coming out from under this rock."

"Wait," another voice called. "I see the stream up here."

"It goes under those trees," Peter Littledove said. "Let's follow it."

The girls in the cave stepped farther back into the shadows. There was a long silence. Rebecca could feel her heart pounding in her chest.

"It goes around this big rock." Peter Littledove's voice sounded very close.

"Yeah, here it is," Mr. Sam said. "That niece of yours is a persistent little thing. Do you think she found it?"

"I don't think she found it, or she would be talking more," Peter replied. "She hasn't been saying much since her arrowheads and pipe disappeared. I think she suspects me, but who cares? Once we get the papers all signed it won't matter."

The mouth of the cave suddenly grew darker as Peter Littledove poked his head into it. If he had looked a few seconds longer, his eyes would have grown used to the darkness and he might have spied the four frightened girls pressed up against the rocks to his left. But instead, he pulled his head out of the opening.

"I doubt if she found this opening," Mr. Sam said. "She probably thought the stream came up out of that rock."

"You're probably right," Peter grunted. "When we saw her before, she was definitely much lower down the hill."

"I'll sure be glad when you get those papers signed this afternoon," Mr. Sam said. "I'm getting tired of playing all those tricks. I hate making little girls cry." He chuckled.

Peter Littledove laughed along with him. "The sooner those three girls leave, the better off we'll be."

"You should have seen their faces when I got those snakes out of the bathroom." Mr. Sam laughed again. "I heard them say they were going to call Mama and go home today."

"I hope you're right," Peter said. "The quicker they go, the sooner everyone forgets about this cave. Then we won't run into any complications."

"Dave and Joe, we're up here!" Mr. Sam shouted. "Bring the charge!"

"We wouldn't be in this mess at all if my father wasn't so stubborn," Peter Littledove said bitterly. "Our family has a chance to make hundreds of thousands of dollars, if not millions, and he stalls and stalls just because he doesn't believe in gambling. That casino will go in somewhere else if we don't jump at this opportunity of a lifetime. That crazy old man could ruin it for the rest of us."

"Put it right up there, boys," Mr. Sam said.

The girls could hear people moving around outside, but they had stopped speaking.

"How long?" a voice asked at last.

"One minute should be enough," Peter Littledove said.

"Will do," the voice replied. The girls heard the scraping sound of metal on rock and then nothing.

"It's ready," the voice said.

"Let's go then," Peter said.

The girls didn't hear any more talking. They waited inside the cave, holding their breath.

"What were they talking about?" Emily whispered. "He said one minute."

"What's that hissing noise?" Rebecca asked.

"A snake?" Emily asked quickly.

"It's not that kind of hiss." Rebecca cocked her head and slowly moved toward the noise, which was getting louder. The other girls followed her. As they crossed over to the opening, they all saw the burning fuse at the same time. It dangled in front of the mouth of the cave, sputtering and sparking as it rapidly grew shorter.

"Dynamite!" Rebecca whispered hoarsely.

"Back into the cave, quick!" Mary said. She ran toward the dark passageway behind them. The other girls were right on her heels. She turned behind the big boulder and kept going into the darkness.

They had just turned the next corner when the dynamite exploded. The noise was deafening. The air in the cave whooshed past them with great force. The ground shook and rocks fell, and everything got dark before the roar echoed into silence.

Chapter Nine

Trapped!

R ebecca was the first one to get her flashlight out of
her backpack and flip it on. The cave was filled
with a thick cloud of dust and smoke. The smell
reminded Rebecca of firecrackers, only it was stronger.

"Are you all right?" Rebecca shined her light on the other
girls. Julie had her hands over her head. Mary Littledove's
face was covered with dirt. Emily sat cross-legged, shaking
her head and rubbing her ears. Rebecca coughed

"That was a close call," Julie said finally.

"Too close," Rebecca said. "I had no idea what they were
talking about."

"When I saw that burning fuse, I thought we were dead,"
Emily said.

"Do you think they were trying to kill us?" Rebecca asked.

"Of course not," Mary Littledove said solemnly. "My
uncle is greedy, but he isn't a murderer. He didn't know we

were in here. He just wanted to make sure no one discovered this cave. Now no one will, I'm afraid."

Her words began to sink in to the other girls. Rebecca stared at her friends fearfully. She flipped the beam of her flashlight in the direction of the mouth of the cave. She hurried quickly back around the corner. As she got to the next bend, she was stopped by a wall of broken rocks, boulders and dirt.

"Help! Help!" she yelled at the wall of rubble.

"They won't be able to hear you," Mary said sadly.

"You mean we're stuck in here?" Rebecca asked.

"Don't say that," Emily replied. "You guys are scaring me."

Julie and Emily got their flashlights out and turned them on. They walked over to the wall of rubble that blocked their escape. Emily picked up a small stone, then dropped it, realizing that there was no way they could dig themselves out. The rocks in front of them weighed hundreds of pounds.

"What will we do?" Emily asked.

"Maybe we can get out of that other hole, the one we first fell into," Rebecca said.

"Are you kidding?" Emily asked.

"Maybe we can find something the Indians left in here and climb up there," Rebecca said with more enthusiasm than she really felt.

"I don't think Native Americans left any aluminum ladders lying around," Emily said glumly.

"You know I don't mean that," Rebecca said.

"Wait. Rebecca may be right," Mary said. "There may be things farther back in the cave that we can use. It's our only hope."

"You mean you want us to go wandering off into this cave?" Emily asked.

"I don't think we have much choice," Julie said without much emotion. "It's clear we aren't leaving the way we came in."

"I'm sorry," Mary Littledove said slowly. "I never thought something like this would happen."

"Why did you bring us here in the first place?" Rebecca demanded irritably.

"I knew no one at the camp believed you," Mary said sadly. "I was trying to help you. And trying to save the camp."

"I still don't understand what's going on here," Julie said. "Can you explain why you ran away when we got back to camp?"

All the flashlights were trained on Mary's face. She squinted in their glare. Julie turned her light off, and then Emily turned hers off.

"We should save our batteries," Julie said. "One flashlight should be enough."

"So what happened, Mary?" Rebecca asked.

"When we got to camp, I thought my grandfather would be in the director's office alone," Mary said. "When I saw Uncle Peter there, I ran away because I'm afraid of him."

"Why?"

"Because he's a mean, greedy man, and he threatened my father, his own brother," Mary said. "Uncle Peter is the one pushing the family to have this land used for a gambling casino. All the other uncles and my two aunts are afraid of him because he is the oldest son."

"A gambling casino?" Rebecca asked. "You mean like those places out in Las Vegas?"

"That's right," Mary said. "Because of new laws and regulations, some Native American tribes and families are eligible to set up gambling casinos on Native American land. The casinos make lots and lots of money, millions of dollars, according to Uncle Peter. He has powerful friends. My father says some of them are criminals. They all want to put a gambling casino up on Moaning Rock Hill. This is an ideal location, according to my uncle. This land is close enough to the highway, and it's up high where everyone can see it from a distance."

"I saw something on the news recently about gambling casinos on Native American lands," Julie said. "Lots of states are opening them."

"Well, some people in my grandfather's family are opposed to them," Mary said. "They have been having big fights for several months now. But my grandfather is growing tired of the bickering. He all but agreed to Uncle Peter's plan last night."

"So why do they want to close up this cave?" Emily asked. "I don't understand."

"You found some things my people made many years ago," Mary said solemnly. "And even the bones of someone. This may be a burial ground. Even if it's not, bones and old tools are protected by law. Once the discovery became known, the tribal government and the federal government would surely want to come and do studies here. They would maybe want to put the pieces in a museum."

"And that would tie up the land, wouldn't it?" Julie said. "They wouldn't allow anyone to build a casino on top of a burial ground or an important site for old objects."

"That's right," Mary said. "These are very important to our people."

"They are important to everyone because they're a part of history," Rebecca added.

"Mr. Sam knows they're important too," Mary said. "As soon as he heard what you all found, he told my uncle. I had hidden the arrowheads and pipe in my suitcase in our camper. I went to the stable to feed Thunder. When I got back, the arrowheads and pipe were gone. I'm sure my uncle took them so it would look like I was lying. Then, later that night, he had Mr. Sam and the construction crew cover up the hole you fell into. He just told the construction crew that it was dangerous for the campers. None of them knew they were covering up the entrance to a cave."

"But Mr. Sam knew it was a cave," Julie said angrily. "And he made such a big deal about driving us up here on the hay-ride wagon. He brought us up here so we would look like fools in front of the whole camp."

"He knew that Shelly and I had argued," Rebecca said. "He must have been the one writing those awful notes."

"What notes?" Mary asked. Rebecca quickly told her about the recent incidents in Firebird Cabin. Mary didn't seemed surprised or shocked. "And so this morning, there were three snakes in the bathroom. Karen said she only saw two, but he mentioned three before he ever went in. So it really was him trying to get us mad and make us feel bad so we would leave the camp."

"That was his plan, because you were the only three that actually were inside the cave and saw the skeleton," Mary said. "Like I said, he is working with Uncle Peter, who promised to give Mr. Sam and his wife good jobs at the casino."

"How do you know that?" Julie asked.

"Because I heard them talking yesterday outside the stables," Mary said. "They were outside. They didn't see me. They've been working together, I guess, ever since Mr. Sam and his wife came to camp. I would have told you sooner, but I was afraid of my uncle. I didn't find the cave entrance until early this morning. I needed help so it wasn't just my word against Uncle Peter. No one would believe a nine-year-old girl instead of the oldest son in the family. I brought you all here because I was hoping we could gather more old tools and take them to my grandfather. All of us together with more proof would convince them. Uncle Peter made fun of me when I tried to tell my aunts and uncles. No one really believed me."

"So that's why you wanted us to bring our backpacks," Julie said.

"Yes, I was sure we could find more," Mary said.

"Now it all makes sense," Rebecca said bitterly. "And to think I was so mad at Shelly when she was innocent just like she claimed all along."

"What an evil man," Julie said. "I can't believe Mr. Sam would actually do something like that."

"He's greedy, just like my uncle," Mary said.

"We have to tell somebody what's going on." Rebecca jumped to her feet and picked up her backpack. The other girls just watched her silently. For a moment Rebecca had forgotten the blast. She looked helplessly at the wall of rocks and rubble.

"We can't just sit here," Emily said.

"It's dangerous to wander around in caves," Julie said.

"But we have no choice," Rebecca replied. "We can follow the stream. It should lead us to the room we fell into, shouldn't it? Maybe we can find old poles or something and climb up to the top of the hole. It's not the same as a ladder, but there might be something we can use."

"But we won't be able to move a steel plate covered with rocks, will we?" Emily asked.

"Can you think of anything better?" Rebecca asked, shining her flashlight from face to face. "Even if we can't move it, we can shout, and maybe they will hear us. They'll be looking for us once they know we're missing."

"But are you sure we can get there?" Emily asked.

"We can follow the stream," Rebecca said. "That way we won't get lost. We have three flashlights."

"Just use one at a time," Julie said.

"Let's go then." Rebecca tightened the straps on her backpack. The other girls did the same. "Are we ready?"

"No, we need to pray." Emily bowed her head. The four girls prayed silently for a long moment.

"Lord, please guide our steps so we can get out of here," Julie said finally.

"Amen," Mary said.

"Let's go." Rebecca shined the light down on the little stream. She began to follow it deeper into the cave. The rest of the girls were right behind her.

The passageway of the cave was quite broad. After about fifteen yards, another passageway broke off from the first. The stream went to the left.

"Stick with the stream," Julie said. "That's our best hope of getting back to that room with the tunnel."

"She's right," Emily added. Rebecca took the passageway to the left. The incline of the cave gradually went higher and higher.

The deeper they went into the cave, the more afraid Rebecca felt. She tried not to show it, however.

"Look at that!" Julie said as they turned a jagged corner. She pointed at the opposite wall.

"Wow!" Emily said. "It looks just like deer."

On the wall in front of them was a old drawing of two deer, a male and female.

"I wonder what they used to make those marks," Rebecca said. "They didn't have spray paint or felt-tipped markers back then."

"It must be soot or some kind of dark stone," Mary replied. "Any kind of drawing is important."

The children kept walking. In the next room were more pictures of animals and people. The girls stared with amazement.

"This is like a regular museum in here." Julie stared at the decorated walls. Rebecca lingered, looking at the pictures.

"These must have been here a long time," Rebecca said softly.

"I wonder if it was just one artist or a whole tribe of artists," Emily added.

The children moved on, always making sure they were following the stream. Another passageway led off to the left, but this time the stream followed the passageway to the right. The four girls followed the stream.

They walked deeper and deeper into the cave. Suddenly they came into a large room that looked familiar. Rebecca shined the light around the walls. A pile of dirt and small rocks was at the far end of the room. Two single sticks were sticking up out of the dirt pile. The tops of the sticks were burnt black.

"This where we fell in, you guys!" Julie said excitedly.

"This is it all right," Rebecca replied. "There's that triangular opening up ahead."

Rebecca shined the light all around the room, hoping to see some kind of pole or tree or anything that would help them get up the long tunnel.

"The bats are still here." Rebecca shined her light on the ceiling. Hundreds of the furry creatures squirmed and squeaked under the glare of the bright flashlight. She ran over to the tunnel. She searched the ground and picked up a long sharp stone.

"Here's the spear point I dropped," Rebecca called out, holding it up so the others could see it. She put the long sharp point in her backpack.

"Let's keep going," Emily said.

The four girls followed the tiny stream through the triangular opening. In the next room, Rebecca turned the flashlight to their right on the skeleton. Mary's eyes opened wide when she saw the collection of white bones.

"You were right." Mary took a deep breath. The four girls went over for a closer look. Rebecca trained the light on the skeleton's chest so Mary could see the spearhead embedded in the bone.

"What's in his hand?" Mary asked.

"I've been wondering about that ever since I saw him," Rebecca replied.

"Should we touch it?" Julie asked.

Mary bent down. She moved one bony finger slightly to the left. Rebecca trained the light on the hand. A piece of skin or something leatherlike was covering the object in the hand. Mary poked it ever so slightly. A golden glint shone up out of the hand. "It's something like gold in its hand."

"You guys, we should leave it alone," Julie said seriously.

"People will want to make a study of this stuff without us having touched it."

"But don't you want to know what it is?" Emily asked.

"Of course I do, but I think we can wait a little longer," Julie said. "We need to find a way up the hole."

"Let's look in the next room." Rebecca stood up. She walked back over to the stream and followed it around the big jutting rock. The big stone table came into view. Rebecca walked farther into the room.

"Wow!" Julie quickly got her flashlight out of her backpack. Emily did the same.

"Do you believe this place?" Rebecca asked. "It's like a Native American department store or something."

The three lights flashed around the walls. Arrowheads, axes, grinders, pipes and all sorts of other things made of stone and bone were lying on every flat surface in the room. Ledges in the walls were filled with all kinds of clay pots. Everywhere they turned there was something new to see.

"There are hundreds of things in here," Mary said solemnly. "This is an important find. I've never seen so many things, even in a museum."

"Me neither," Rebecca said breathlessly. "Look over there. More bones." The four girls saw hundreds of bones in a smaller room off the big room.

"I wonder if those are human bones or animal bones," Rebecca said. "Maybe that was their dump."

"Look for poles or long sticks that we can use to climb out of here," Julie said.

"I don't see anything like that," Rebecca said.

"Me neither," Julie replied. The girls kept walking along the stream. When they got to the far end of the room, the stream ended, or rather started. The water bubbled up out of a hole and collected in a shallow pool in the rock floor about as deep as a bathtub and five feet across. At the far end of the pool, the water spilled out and began running downhill.

"This is where the spring starts," Julie said. "I guess water has been bubbling up out of here for hundreds of years."

"It's like having indoor plumbing," Emily said.

"I don't see anything that's going to help us get up that tunnel," Rebecca said with discouragement. Even with all the wonder of discovery, she realized that none of it would mean anything if they were trapped in the cave. The thought was too awful to think about. She shined her light up at the ceiling. Two bats squeaked and dropped away from the rock.

"Bats!" Emily yelled. The girls aimed their flashlights up. The bats swirled and dived erratically in the air of the large room. One of the furry creatures dipped very close to Rebecca's head. She screamed.

The bat jerked back up into the air and headed out over the pool, disappearing around the far corner of the room. The other bat followed its companion. Rebecca aimed her light up in the corner of the cave where the bats had disappeared. She was afraid they would return.

"They're gone," Emily said with relief.

Julie kept shining her light in the corner where they had last seen the bats. She walked toward it.

"Remember that day we fell down in the other room?" Julie asked.

"What happened?" Mary asked.

"They all took off at once," Julie said. "The air was filled with bats."

"Yeah, I thought they were going to attack us," Rebecca

said. "They flew around for a while. Then like on command, they all flew out through that triangular passageway."

"That means they must have flown through here," Julie said. "Like those other two bats."

"So what?" Rebecca asked.

"Don't you see?" Julie said. "Bats fly outside. Didn't you ever go to Carlsbad Caverns and watch the bats come out in the evening? They come out by the thousands. The air gets dark with them."

"I see what you're saying," Emily added. "You're wondering where those two bats went. They didn't follow the stream and leave by the entrance we came in today or through the tunnel we fell down."

"Then you mean . . ."

"There must be another way out," Rebecca said. "The bats have to go outside some way."

"And maybe we can get out the same way!" Mary said.

"Let's go find those bats!" Julie exclaimed. The four girls almost ran around the pool of water.

"I thought the cave ended in this room," Rebecca said, "just because the stream ended here."

"It looks like it ends, but there's a passageway ahead of us. See?" Julie said. "The bats must have flown through there."

Once they got beyond the pool of water at the end of the room, it was easier to see the narrow passageway. When they entered it and shined their lights, it looked like a long stone hallway over thirty yards long. The girls walked single file as fast as they could go.

"Slow down!" Julie warned Rebecca, who was in the lead. "You don't want to fall down a hole."

Rebecca stopped. For a moment, it looked like the long

narrow passageway came to a dead end. Rebecca could feel her hope sinking. But when she got to the very end, there was another narrow passageway to her right. She turned and went about five yards before the passageway turned again and opened up into a small room. That's when she saw a patch of blue sky not ten feet away. "I can see sky, you guys!"

The others crowded up around her into the small room. The blue sky shone bright and clear right in front of them through an oblong opening about two feet wide and five feet high.

Rebecca poked her head outside. The others were close behind her. Mary led the way.

"We're on the other side of Moaning Rock Hill," Mary said. "But this entrance is hidden by these big boulders, because it comes out at such a strange angle. You'd almost have to fall down here to find this opening."

"We made it!" Rebecca had a huge smile on her face.

"Not yet!" Mary said. "We still have work to do. We have to get to my grandfather before he signs any papers. We have to take him evidence."

"You're right," Rebecca said seriously. "We'll help you. Wait until they see some of the things we can show them."

Mary turned and went back into the cave. The other girls followed her. In the distance, a boom filled the air and the ground trembled.

Chapter Ten

Making History

More than a dozen cars were parked around the Littledove ranch house at noontime. Mary Littledove, Rebecca, Julie, Emily, Karen and Janet walked hurriedly along the wooden rail by the house. Each girl was wearing a backpack. As they climbed up on the big porch, a bright red Jeep sped up the driveway and came to a rough halt. Dust filled the air.

Peter Littledove bounded up the steps with a smile. When he saw Mary, he stopped smiling, but only for an instant.

"I see you found your friends, Mary." Her uncle stopped by the front door, blocking it.

"I need to see my grandfather," Mary said.

"We are having an important meeting today, Mary," her uncle said. "You'll have to wait until we're through."

"I don't have time," Mary insisted.

"I'm sure her grandfather will want to hear what Mary has to say," Janet said. The tall man looked at the counselor with a steely expression.

"This is family business, children." Peter's eyes narrowed. "You'll have to come back later."

"Mary!" a voice said behind the screen door. Her grandmother pushed open the door. "Why don't you and your friends come inside?"

"Mother, we don't have time for these children," Peter Littledove insisted.

"Nonsense," the old woman said. "Mary and her friends are welcome here."

"But Mother!" the tall man protested. Mrs. Littledove stared at him.

"This is my home, Peter," she said firmly. Mary rushed through the doorway. She gave her grandmother a hug. Rebecca and the others followed Mary into the house. Peter Littledove was right behind them.

Mary ran into the living room. Over two dozen men and women were gathered in the room, sitting in chairs, dressed in suits or fancy dresses. Mr. Sam sat in the corner of the room. Grandfather Littledove sat at the front of the room in a big chair. He wore a dark blue suit. A small table covered with papers was in front of the old man. He looked up at Mary with tired eyes.

"Don't sign anything, Grandfather!" Mary almost shouted. "You must see what we found in a cave on Moaning Rock Hill."

"There is no cave on Moaning Rock Hill," Peter said loudly. "Let's quit wasting time. You've made the right decision, Father. Let's finish this business and celebrate an important day, a day of history in the Littledove family."

The old man held up his hand to silence his son. Peter Littledove began to pace back and forth.

"Look what we found, Grandfather." Mary motioned to the other girls. All of them quickly took off their heavy backpacks and opened them. Each girl began laying out pieces of pottery, ax heads, figurines, spear points and other stone treasures on the floor in the middle of the room. The other people in the room began to whisper.

"Look at all these things," Mary said. "And this is only part of what we found. There are hundreds more in the cave. There is even a skeleton and maybe the graves of our ancestors."

"I've already called the state historical society and the anthropology department at our university." Janet Crowe smiled. "They think this could be a major find."

"These are not Cherokee," the old man said.

Janet nodded in agreement. "They appear older. Moaning Rock sits on top of one of the richest archaeological finds in this state."

Peter Littledove slumped down into a chair and rubbed his face with his hands. The other people in the room began talking loudly. Grandfather Littledove smiled. He stacked the papers in front of him into a pile. Then he placed the pile of papers in a folder and closed it. He stood up.

"History has been made today as surely as you have spoken," the old man said to his son. "We do have reason to celebrate. I will not let this land be used to rob others like our people were robbed. I will not sign these papers."

Mary ran across the room and hugged her grandfather. The old man smiled as he hugged her back.

Chapter Eleven

Stories
at the
Campfire

The next night, all the girls were gathered around a circle of burning logs. Each girl was trying to cook her own hot dog. The food at camp hadn't been quite as good as when Miss Minnie and Mr. Sam made it, but no one cared that the couple was gone. Once Mr. Harvey found out who was responsible for the mean pranks in Firebird Cabin, he fired Mr. Sam on the spot. As it turned out, Miss Minnie knew all about the pranks too. She had written the first two notes and had poured the syrup.

But that already seemed like ancient history. The big fire was hot, and the smell of cooking hot dogs filled the air. The Firebird Cabin girls and the Coyote Cabin girls sat in a big circle by the baseball field near third base. Shelly and Bernice sat right next to Rebecca.

"Wait till you see that skeleton," Rebecca said. "I thought it was really creepy at first, but once you get used to it, it's more sad than anything else. And you should see what it's holding in its hand. It's a figurine of a bird, sort of like an eagle. Maybe it's even a firebird, like the name of our cabin."

"Only it appears to be made of solid gold!" Emily added. "That's why Mr. Littledove has hired guards at the entrance of the cave. They will be there until the state historical society comes and starts their studies."

"Will they really let us go into the cave?" Shelly asked hopefully.

"Janet says we can go in, one cabin at a time, if we don't touch anything," Rebecca said. "Old Mr. Littledove has given us permission. Janet says several different agencies will come in at the end of this session in a few days and begin their studies. Coach Linnell says that maybe they'll add cave spelunking to the camp activities."

"You guys will really become famous," Bernice said proudly.

"We didn't really do anything but fall down a hole," Rebecca said.

"I wouldn't say that's all you did," Bernice replied. "I would have lost my nerve once they exploded that dynamite that covered up the entrance."

"You know, Dave, the construction foreman, said he thinks it was all the blasting that opened up the hole we found in the first place," Julie said. "So in a way, it was good that they had started building that new road. If they hadn't, we would never have found the cave at all."

"They can still use the road," Emily said. "Janet thinks that they might make the cave some kind of natural history museum someday. Camp Friendly Waters will really become famous then."

After dinner, the girls gathered around the big fire. Grandfather Littledove walked slowly across the field, holding hands with Mary. Everyone clapped when he sat down near the fire on a big worn rock. Mary sat beside him.

As the fire burned bright, the old man began to tell stories of the Cherokee. The girls heard about victories and defeats. They heard about promises and betrayals. Finally, they heard about a trail of tears over a thousand miles long. The children listened with great attention. They listened to the old stories just as children had done for hundreds of years, gathered around fires out under the stars. With the discovery of the cave on Moaning Rock Hill, history seemed more alive than ever as the old man talked.

Sparks jumped up into the night, and the air got cool. Rebecca and Shelly huddled next to each other to keep warm. Shelly smiled as her new friend moved closer. It seemed as if Camp Friendly Waters was living up to its name at last.

**Don't miss the next book
in the Home School Detectives
series!**

**Here's a preview of
John Bibee's
*The Mystery at
the Broken Bridge***

Chapter One

Basketball Steal

The Good Friday picnic at the Bridgewood Apartments was going well until Josh Morgan discovered that his brand-new basketball was missing. He had bought the basketball with money he had worked for and saved over several months. It was official size and weight with a real leather cover. He had brought it to the workday/cookout so he and the other kids could play at the new backboard that had been set up that morning.

"I can't believe those guys took it," Josh said angrily after he finished eating the last bit of his hamburger. He glared at the group of kids hanging out under the broken bridge near the Bridgewood Apartments. He knew some of their names, but that was about all he knew. The kids under the bridge were eating hamburgers and hot dogs and seemed totally unaware of Josh's anger. They were laughing and joking with one another.

"They act like nothing even happened," Carlos Brown said.

"Yeah," Billy Renner agreed. "We're out here trying to do something nice, and these guys steal from us."

"You don't know for a fact that they took it," Julie Brown said softly.

"Of course they took it," Josh said bitterly. "It didn't just dribble off by itself. Carlos and Billy and I looked everywhere: down in the creek bed, in the hedges."

"Did you look under the broken bridge?" Julie asked.

"I especially looked around under there," Josh said. "It's just gone."

"Yeah," Carlos agreed. "It's gone. Long gone."

"And they said that none of them took it or saw anything," Billy said. "It makes me really mad. I think we should go interrogate each one and see who is lying. If we put the pressure on, I bet they'll confess." Billy Renner jumped up off the picnic bench to start the investigation.

"Hold on." His twin sister, Rebecca, pulled her brother back down to his place on the picnic bench. The others nodded in approval. Billy was always quick on the trigger when it came to doing anything that was remotely interesting to him, especially if it had to do with solving a mystery.

"But we're the Home School Detectives," Billy said. "People expect us to solve mysteries. So let's go. This is Josh's ball. I think we need to put the pressure on, and they'll spill their guts."

"Hang on, Sherlock." Rebecca grabbed her brother by the back of his shirt again. Billy sat down, a frown on his face.

"You haven't even finished eating."

The other kids at the picnic table nodded. They all knew about Billy's impulsive side because all of them had raced to keep up with it at one time or another. In two seconds he had forgotten that just a minute before he was talking about how hungry he was and saying that he could eat three hamburgers. He had settled for two burgers, a huge stack of potato chips and two cans of soda. But he was ready to forget his hunger as soon as he started thinking about how to get the basketball back. The others had already finished their food, but Billy wasn't done because he had been talking while the others were eating.

The six young people, Josh and Emily Morgan, Billy and Rebecca Renner, and Julie and Carlos Brown, had been known as the Home School Detectives around Springdale ever since they had helped the police solve a thirty-year-old mystery involving a robbery and hidden treasure. Since that time, they had solved a number of mysteries and gained a reputation for being effective detectives.

"What did your dad say about your basketball?" Julie asked sympathetically.

"He said that maybe it will turn up," Josh said in disgust.

"Well, maybe it will." Emily felt sorry for her brother and for herself too, because she and Josh shot baskets at home. They had a hoop out in front of their house by the driveway. Now they would have to use the old basketball, which was already worn and smooth from so much use.

"I know someone stole it," Josh fumed. "I never should have let those bridge kids use it."

"Yeah, I bet they know what really happened," Billy said. "They're just lying to protect each other."

"But they might not have taken it," Julie insisted softly. "You guys really shouldn't accuse people without knowing the facts."

"What do you mean?" Josh demanded. "I let them use it while we were working inside, cleaning out the rec room. They stole it and you know it."

"But Ricky Carson said he set it down by the barbecue grill when they lined up to get hamburgers," Julie said.

"That's what he claims," Josh said with contempt. "He could be lying to protect himself if he's the thief."

"But what if he is telling the truth?" Julie asked.

"Ricky said that when they got up near the grill to get their food, they noticed that the basketball was gone," Rebecca added. "Someone could have taken it, but it could have been anyone. It might have been someone from our church and not the kids out here."

"None of our church friends would steal my basketball," Josh said. "Do you really believe that?"

"I don't," Billy said. "How can you accuse people in your own church of doing something like that without any facts?"

"Well, Josh is accusing the Bridgewood kids without any facts," Julie said.

"But they had the basketball last," Josh almost yelled. "That is a fact, and in my mind that makes them the prime suspects." He propped his elbows on the picnic table and looked at the Bridgewood Apartment kids with disgust. Everyone seemed to be having a good time but Josh.

"All I'm saying is that it's not fair to accuse *all* the Bridgewood kids of taking your ball," Julie said. "Maybe one of them took it, but it sounds like you're accusing all of them, and you can't lump people together like that."

"Well, Josh could be right," Billy said. "Some people say there are gangs over on this side of town. If they're a gang, they'd stick up for each other and lie for each other. So they would be in it together."

"Yeah, they could be in gangs and be lying," Josh said.

"But you still don't know that for sure," Julie countered. She sighed. "It's too bad. Everything was going well. My dad is really excited about all the things getting done around here today. Mr. Gossett, the owner of the apartments, is really happy. At first my dad said Mr. Gossett was suspicious about us coming out here to help. But now that he's gotten to know us, he's really helping out. Opening up the storage room as a recreation room and buying the Ping-Pong table was really nice of him."

"The Ping-Pong table is great," Emily agreed. "It's brand-new."

There were all sorts of people from the Springdale Community Church out that Friday afternoon around the Bridgewood Apartment complex, doing all kinds of work to make the apartments and surroundings a nicer place to live. Some were carrying paint cans and paintbrushes. Others had shovels and rakes. Some were still inside working on the apartments. The six children had been helping cut the grass and pull weeds and clean the new recreation room.

The Bridgewood Apartments were known as a place where lower-income people lived. There were several old people living in the apartments, as well as many young single mothers and lots of children. Mary Kline, one of the young mothers living in the apartments, was a friend of Louise Jones, who was a member of the Springdale Community Church. When Mary's water heater broke and she was told she would have to wait a week to get it fixed, Mary told Louise her problem. Louise then asked some of the men in the church to help Mary. The next day two men and two boys from the church went to Mary's apartment and replaced her water heater. She was so excited and thankful that she told Mrs. Perkins and Mrs. May, two older women across the hallway. As it turned out, they needed help with their plugged-up sink and dripping faucet. After the church group helped them, they realized there were lots of people in the apartments who could use help with one thing or another. Some of the older people, for instance, had lights that were out, but they were too old to get up on ladders and change the bulbs.

The outside of the apartments was rundown and messy. There was a play area for the children, with a swing set and slide, but all of the swings were missing. The merry-go-round didn't turn, and the steps to the slide were broken. At one time there had been a basketball hoop set up on a small cement court, but all that was left was a bare pole; the backboard had been gone for years. The yard around the apartments was full of weeds and spots of bare dirt. Several walls had been spray painted with graffiti. The asphalt parking lot and sidewalks were also decorated by spray-painted messages and pictures.

Even the old bridge near the apartments was falling down and dangerous to walk on. It was a large wooden footbridge that crossed a creek. On the other side of the creek was a small park. Beyond the park were the Gateway Apartments, which were also in poor shape, but not as bad as the Bridgewood Apartments.

The old broken bridge was a popular place, even though it was falling apart. Lots of young people hung out under the bridge in the creek bed; most of them lived in the Bridgewood or Gateway apartments. The kids who hung out there had a bad reputation around town. Lots of people referred to them as the "the bridge kids." Most people assumed the graffiti sprayed on the walls of the Bridgewood Apartments came from them. Some people said they were members of gangs, though others said Springdale was too small to have gangs. Others said the bridge kids used drugs. There were lots of empty beer cans under the old bridge.

Several young people were down by the bridge talking and eating. They seemed to be having a good time. Josh looked at the group of kids with suspicion and disgust. Some were sitting on bicycles. Others were on foot. One girl was wearing in-line skates.

"I should have figured something like this would happen," Josh said. "I should have known not to bring my ball."

"You couldn't have known your ball would get stolen," Julie said.

"But I did know there is more crime in this part of town." Josh was still looking at the kids near the bridge.

"Why do you suppose that is?" Billy asked. "I mean, poorer people live here. It seems like there would be less to steal. You'd think thieves would go to the richer parts of town to steal things."

"They steal around our house too," Emily said. "I heard my mom talking with old Mrs. Harrington on the phone. She lives at the end of our street in that big old house. She said she was missing things out of her garage. I think she said a Weed-Eater is gone and something else."

"There is a regular crime wave in Springdale." Billy jumped up with excitement. "I say it calls for us to break this case right now. Let's go!"

"Sit down!" the other kids said loudly in unison.

"You guys are no fun." Billy, clearly disappointed, lowered himself to the bench again.

"I do want to ask a few more questions," Josh said to the others.

"What do you mean?" Emily saw that her brother was staring at the kids over by the bridge again. "Do you really think the bridge kids did it?"

"Well, I don't know about Mrs. Harrington's Weed-Eater, but I do think at least one of them stole my basketball," Josh said. "They have a reputation around town for causing lots of trouble."

"Let's go interrogate the suspects," Billy said.

"I think it's a mistake to go over there and accuse them," Julie said. "You want to start a fight?"

"I'm not going to start a fight," Josh replied. "But I'm not going to back down either. I want my ball back."

"We better go together," Carlos advised. "Those are tough kids. They get in fights a lot. I heard one of the moms telling my dad that she was afraid her son was getting involved in some kind of gang. She said he left home whenever he felt like it and would be gone for a long time."

"That doesn't mean he is in a gang," Emily said.

"Well, I'm just saying that this mom thought her son was in a gang," Carlos said.

"Who was it?" Billy asked curiously.

"I can't tell you," Carlos said. "I mean, my parents don't want us to talk about church stuff or things we overhear. They say that's gossip."

"Gossip?" Billy asked. "That's not gossip. That's just information. We're trying to find out who stole Josh's ball.

We're detectives on a case."

"Carlos is right," Julie said. "Our dad told us not to talk about stuff like that. He tries to keep private matters private, but sometimes we can't help but overhear things. I know who Carlos is referring to, but it wouldn't be right to talk about him."

"Well, can we go over to the bridge and at least check things out?" Billy asked.

"All I want to do is ask a few more questions." Josh stood up.

"But I'm not finished eating!" Billy yelled out as his attention suddenly shifted back to his hunger.

"That's because you talk too much," Rebecca said flatly.

"We'll go dump our plates and trash," Josh said to Billy. "We'll come back for you."

While Josh and the others picked up their paper plates, Billy hurriedly stuffed the remaining potato chips into his mouth. He chewed anxiously as he watched his friends walk away. He took a big gulp of orange soda, hoping to make the chips go down faster. He stuffed in the last bite of hamburger.

"I'm done!" Billy hopped up and followed his friends. After they dumped their paper plates and cups in a big green garbage bag, they walked across the newly cleaned basketball court. Josh looked up at the new backboard, the orange rim and bright white net.

"I only got to shoot one basket out here today," Josh said as they walked by the hoop.

"Maybe your basketball will turn up," Julie said. "Why don't we look around together before you go talk to those kids? You shouldn't go over there if you're mad."

"I have a right to be mad," Josh said. "My basketball is missing."

The kids under the broken bridge stopped talking as they saw Josh and his friends come down the creek bank. The old bridge was covered with bright spray-painted names and symbols. The largest picture of all was a large blue cross painted on a metal reinforcement plate on the side of the bridge. Underneath someone had spelled the name Jesus, with the letter *S* written backwards.

"Hey, Ricky," Josh said without smiling.

"You find your ball yet?" Ricky Carson asked.

"No," Josh said glumly.

"I'm sure sorry about that," Ricky replied. "But I told you where I put it. None of us have seen it since then." The other kids nodded in agreement. Josh searched their faces.

"That ball cost me a lot of money," Josh said slowly. "I saved a long time to get it."

"I don't know what else to tell you," Ricky said.

"Those Gateway kids might have taken it," a tall boy named Chester said. "They're a bunch of thieves."

"Yeah, it could be them," Ricky agreed. "They like to come over here and cause trouble. They paint on our bridge."

"Yeah." Chester pointed to a black spray-painted scrawl above his head. "You see that? That's their Gateway letter *G* near the big blue cross."

Josh squinted at the picture. At first he didn't see it because the letter was so zigzagged and square-looking.

"It does look sort of like a *G* if you look at it the right way," Julie said.

"Yeah, that's their sign," Ricky said. "They come over here and try to cause trouble. They do it all the time. But we run them off. We protect what's ours. This bridge is ours."

The other kids under the bridge nodded their heads and

looked angry. Some of them were whispering.

"You guys were the last to have Josh's ball," Billy said suspiciously. "And I haven't seen any of the Gateway kids over here."

"Are you accusing me, shorty?" Chester Tucker asked. Like Billy, he was African-American. He wore gray shorts, a dirty gray T-shirt and dirty white basketball shoes. He was at least a foot taller than Billy.

"We aren't accusing anyone, Chester," Julie said nervously.

"You sound like you're calling us thieves." Ricky stood up straighter. He was older and a few inches taller than Josh. His eyes had grown hard suddenly. "I told you what happened. That's the truth."

"I thought I saw that big guy from your church pick it up," said the girl wearing the in-line skates. "Isn't his name Robert or something?"

"You mean Albert Williams?" Josh asked. "He didn't take my ball. He's a friend of ours."

"So you *are* accusing us," Ricky said defiantly. "Everyone always accuses us of stuff we don't do. Those Gateway kids blame stuff on us, and now you church people are blaming us."

"Yeah," Chester echoed. "Why don't you church kids just get out of here and go back to church?"

"We only came out here today to help you all," Julie said.

"Well, I didn't ask you for no help." Ricky pointed his finger at Josh's chest. "And I didn't ask you to bring your stupid basketball. You gave it to us to play with. If I knew you were going to call me and my friends thieves just because—"

"I didn't call you thieves," Josh replied angrily. "All I'm trying to do is—"

"You sound like you're saying we're thieves." Chester took a few steps forward and stood by Ricky's side. Two other boys walked out from under the bridge and stood next to their friends. All four boys glared angrily at Josh and Billy. Josh took a deep breath, feeling anger and fear well up in his chest. The air was tense and getting worse.

A scream split the air. Everyone stopped talking. Over by the barbecue grill, a woman began to cry out loudly.

"That's my mom!" Ricky sprinted up the creek bank and ran for his mother. Ricky's friends scrambled after him.

"Let's see what's going on." Josh ran after Ricky and the other kids.

By the time Josh arrived at the barbecue grill, a small crowd had gathered around Ms. Carson, who was still crying. She pulled up the apron she was wearing to wipe her eyes. She had been helping serve the hamburgers and hot dogs. Pastor Brown, Julie and Carlos's father, was standing next to the upset woman.

"What's wrong?" Josh asked Chester.

"I don't know," he said with concern.

"It was right here a minute ago," Ms. Carson sobbed to Pastor Brown. "But now it's gone. Someone stole my purse, and it had my rent money in it. What am I going to do?" The woman cried again and pulled her son close to her side.

Also by John Bibee
THE SPIRIT FLYER SERIES

During the course of a year, the ordinary town of Centerville
becomes the setting for some extraordinary events.
When several children discover that Spirit Flyer bicycles
possess strange and wondrous powers, they are thrust
into a conflict with Goliath Industries—with the
fate of the town in the balance.

Book 1 *The Magic Bicycle*
Book 2 *The Toy Campaign*
Book 3 *The Only Game in Town*
Book 4 *Bicycle Hills*
Book 5 *The Last Christmas*
Book 6 *The Runaway Parents*
Book 8 *The Journey of Wishes*

Available from your local bookstore or

InterVarsity Press
Downers Grove, Illinois 60515